Field Fare

by

Mirabelle Maslin

Augur Press

FIELD FARE
Copyright © Mirabelle Maslin 2011

The moral right of the author has been asserted

Author of:
Beyond the Veil
Tracy
Carl and other writings
Fay
On a Dog Lead
Emily
The Fifth Key
The Candle Flame
The Supply Teacher's Surprise
Miranda
Lynne

British Library Cataloguing in Publication Data.
A catalogue record for this book is available from the British Library.

ISBN 978-0-9558936-8-1

First published 2012 by
Augur Press
Delf House,
52, Penicuik Road,
Roslin,
Midlothian EH25 9LH
United Kingdom

Printed by Lightning Source

Field Fare

To all readers who enjoy my writing

Chapter One

Philip Thornton was the only child of a couple who had lived out their days in a small flat in the suburbs of London. They had had to scrimp and save to make ends meet, but they had always prided themselves on the fact that they had managed to get Philip into a good school.

Philip had never married. He rented accommodation that was modest but pleasant, and travelled each day by bus to his job as an office administrator. After working hard all day, he would walk home and then relax, concentrating his mind entirely on his own thoughts and interests.

One day, a letter arrived that disturbed his habitual routine. It contained the kind of information that he had always assumed belonged entirely to fiction. However, in this case it was obviously real. A distant relative on his mother's side had died, leaving a substantial amount of money, and he was the only beneficiary.

It took Philip a long time to take in this news. It took even longer to realise that he could make changes to his life.

Eventually he made his first decision. He would take driving lessons and buy a car. Everything else would stay the same, except that all the time he was now aware that there was a considerable sum of money in his bank account.

The house was situated about a mile along a small lane in some of the best countryside in Cheshire. The building was about 150 years old, and had originally been a large farmhouse, which in its heyday had been the busy hub of a thriving business. The ownership had been handed down through generations of the same family – the Houghtons. However, the last farming couple there had struggled to make a living. They had had several children, none of whom had shown any interest in modernisation of the farm and developing initiatives that would turn round the fortunes of the family. One by one they had moved away to find employment elsewhere. The ageing parents eventually sold off nearly all of their land. It was split into several lots, many of which were purchased by a number of wealthy people to use for their horses. Most of the farm buildings were demolished, and although the outbuildings for the house were retained, the structure of them deteriorated quite quickly as Mr and Mrs Houghton grew older.

As the situation changed, the couple's hearts were no longer in the house that had once been their much loved home. It had been the centre of their life. As their workplace and the place where they had reared their family, it had given them much happiness, but now they lived quietly in only a few of the many rooms. The end came when Mrs Houghton caught her foot in a torn piece of carpet at the top of the stairs and fell awkwardly, breaking several bones. Mr Houghton had then insisted that they moved to sheltered housing, but he could never face the task of selling his house, and he blocked all attempts that his children made to persuade him.

The Houghtons were not long dead when Philip first stumbled upon the house. As far as he was concerned, it was love at first sight. It was a pure accident that he had been driving around in the locality the day the 'For Sale' sign went up.

He had been travelling from the Lake District back to his flat in London, when he had a sudden urge to leave the motorway and do some exploring. Long hours of driving were always lonely and were inevitably boring, and he wanted to fill some time with a variety of inconsequential chat and some good scenery. Once off the motorway, he did not bother to consult a map. If necessary he could find somewhere to stay for the night, and then finish his journey the following day.

A turn down an entirely unprepossessing lane had changed

2

everything. This dilapidated building *had* to be the base of the next phase of his life! Immediately his head filled with plans... He had phoned the agent straight away and insisted that someone came immediately to let him see round the house. While he waited, he had strolled round the outside of it, peering in through the grimy windows. Then he had investigated the outbuildings as well, carefully picking his way through the crumbling mess.

Within weeks a deal had been struck. The excitement Philip felt on that day was beyond anything he had ever experienced before in his life. Straight away he employed a firm of architects and engaged in many intense discussions about the massive task of renovation and refurbishment, which would include extending the house at the back with a rather special conservatory, and converting the outbuildings. He had known right from the beginning that it was to be a hotel of modest size, snug and discreet. Its position, away from close neighbours and prying eyes, was ideal. It was far enough from habitation, but not so far that it would be a nuisance when needing to access essential services.

Every day his mind was full of his plans, and every night he dreamed of their fruition.

Chapter Two

Since the day he had taken over the site, Philip had worked tirelessly with the architects, builders and interior designers, and all his hard work had converted it into a place where he could then set about building up a remarkable business – which he proudly named *Field Fare*.

The dining room was open to non-residents, and customers came from far and wide to experience the fine cuisine. Places had to be pre-booked, as every one of the forty seats was invariably filled. The curious thing was that Philip never advertised his services. People knew of *Field Fare* mainly by word of mouth. News of it had spread so quickly that promotion had never been necessary. Game was his speciality – local rabbit, hare, grouse, pheasant, partridge, pigeon... The list was extensive, as was the variety of soups, terrines and other dishes in which these meats featured. Wild salmon and brown trout were also plentiful at his tables, and he provided fine wines from a well-stocked cellar to complement each dish.

Philip was nearly always on the premises. By day, he wore casual clothes – an open-necked shirt, with impeccably clean trousers and suede shoes. As he entertained his guests in the evenings, his 'country' evening wear was immaculately presented. One remarkable feature of this attire was that he always wore a cravat of a strikingly unusual pattern. He had many of these, and each had a tale attached to it. Diners would press him for the story of the cravat of that evening, and they never went away unsatisfied.

Philip's cultured accent and extensive knowledge of an apparently inexhaustible range of fascinating subjects made him an ideal *maître d'hôtel*. Coupled with his flawlessly courteous manner, one could only assume that he had come from a very good background.

Although Philip was very personable, no one knew him well. He lived alone in rooms to the rear of the upper floor. He was a man of precise habits. His short greying hair was never out of place, his teeth were well kept and well polished, and his meticulously clean nails were always trimmed short. It was difficult to guess his age. He could have been in his mid to late fifties, but he might have been older. Carrying no extra weight, he was in good trim. His skin was that of a younger man, but there were parts of his demeanour that belonged to someone who had experienced more years of life. There was occasionally a hint of the smell of his shaving soap in the air, and to the astute observer this might have provided a clue.

He was known to all the local people to be of a kind and generous nature – offering the use of rooms in his premises for meetings of the Women's Craft Group and other local events for only a modest fee. He treated his staff well, and always trained them to a good standard. Those who did not live locally were offered comfortable accommodation in the sensitively converted outbuildings. These units were largely used by younger members of staff, many of whom were temporary.

The Victorian-style conservatory added to the back of the hotel was exquisite. Philip had taken great care about its design, and also in the choice and layout of the furniture and decorative plants. Although most of the seating was placed centrally for diners, there were particular places amongst the vegetation where guests could sit unobserved and conduct private conversations.

There were five double bedrooms for residents, each of which had a well-presented *en suite* bathroom and wonderful views from their large windows. There had been occasions when Philip had been asked to take a booking for the use of all the facilities for a wedding venue, but he had always declined. This puzzled people who knew, but they made no comment.

Another remarkable attraction of Philip's hotel was that visitors could enjoy viewing the large collection of farmhouse recipes from bygone years that he had amassed. These were displayed in a small room off the substantial entrance hall, and also in two alcoves in the dining room.

Chapter Three

In his core Philip was an admirer of women. More accurately, he was an admirer of himself in relation to women, although any such admiration had to take place in complete secret, and was never apparent in his public life. Before the existence of *Field Fare*, Philip had had no real outlet for this, and when he looked back, he felt that his former life had been cruelly stunted as a result. It was indeed fortunate that over the last three years or so, his admiring opportunities had become more obvious to him, and in this new context his energies had begun to open out in an unusual way. He knew that without *Field Fare* this surely could never have happened.

It had all started with the early planning of the restoration of the main building. During the many hours that Philip had spent examining every part of his future home and place of business, he had come across an anomaly that had puzzled him. There was a section of the upper floor, adjacent to a large chimney stack, that did not seem to fit with external measurements. At first he passed it off as a quirk in the construction that made it seem so, but each time he tried to push it aside, the question in his mind became more forceful. In the end he decided to settle it once and for all by spending an afternoon there, armed with a long measuring tape. This confirmed that his instinct and observations had been correct.

After much careful scrutiny, he eventually found a low panel in the adjacent wall that had a hollow ring to it when tapped briskly. Loosening it with a hammer revealed a dark space beyond. The use of a torch showed a bare room, about ten feet square, with no window. A small amount of dusty clutter suggested that the space had many years previously been used as a store room and had been forgotten long ago. Its gloomy airless state could have been compared with a mausoleum, or even a tomb, but this did not impact adversely on Philip's mood.

The following night, Philip had a glorious dream. The space had been converted into a sumptuous room – full of soft furnishings of satin materials of wonderful colours. There was only one piece of furniture in it – a bed that was covered in sheets of white satin.

From then on, Philip's thoughts and dreams were filled with ideas and plans for that room. Whatever else he was doing, his mind was also occupied with these very private desires. He realised that his own rooms were situated very closely and maybe even next to the secret room. Further investigation revealed that it might be possible to have a connection to it through his bathroom. Whom could he involve to help him to achieve this aim? It was clear that he could not do the necessary alterations himself.

Then he happened upon an idea, and the more he thought about it, the happier he felt. He would let the architect and builder know that he wanted to adapt the room so that he could use it as a small private observatory. He became very excited at the prospect of organising this. The ceiling would be made entirely of glass – a glass dome, perhaps. Strangely, the roof above the room was flat, almost as if it had been designed specifically for the impending conversion. How wonderful it would be to lie with his arms around a female art form, at the same time gazing up to the night sky, watching wisps of cloud trailing across the face of the moon! This space was certainly not to do with death. It was linked strongly in Philip's mind to a voyage of discovery.

His mind made up, Philip put his plans in front of the architect, who was impressed by the details of the telescope he claimed that he would purchase. He could install a bed in there later, when all the workmen had finished. The satin furnishings would be quite easy to collect unobtrusively.

Chapter Four

The day when the First Woman had presented herself was a day that Philip would never forget. It was almost exactly nine months after his 'observatory' had been completed. Before that time, such beings had dwelled only in his fantasy. Lying in his satin-adorned room, he had often imagined them, but until that day he had never met one. This Woman's face seemed to have an ethereal glow. Her name was Carol, and she had come for a cleaning job that he had advertised at the local post office. He had been sufficiently disturbed by her presence that he had feigned a mistake about the interview time, and had asked her to return the following day instead.

That night he lay fully clothed on the bed in his special room, imagining what it would be like if she were there with him. The full moon beamed through the glass at him, and it had a wisp of cloud trailing across it perfectly. The whole experience was so blissful and fulfilling that he decided it would spoil it if someone else were there.

When Carol came again the next day, she was not after all the person he remembered from the day before. He gave her the job, and she became indistinct, merging into the workforce as a cog in a machine.

However, that first encounter with Carol had opened something up for Philip. It had certainly enhanced his appreciation of his time spent in his secret room. She herself was not special to him, but his room was even more special than it had been before.

Apart from that room, Philip's accommodation was quite utilitarian. The entrance to his ordinary bedroom was a door with a number 7 on it. He always kept this door securely locked, and only he had the keys. Immediately inside was a tiny lobby. This ensured that any passer-by could not glance into his private space. Number 7 was a smallish room containing a single bed, a chest of drawers and a wardrobe, and it had a bathroom off it. His other room was a sitting room with a pleasant window out to the back, which was draped with thin net curtaining. A substantial sideboard stood against one wall. There was a large rug on the floor in the middle of the room, and there was a pleasant electric fire in one corner. This room could be made very snug. When Philip was not on show in the hotel, he liked to linger by the window and watch the shapes of guests who were sitting in the conservatory below, members of staff coming and going from their accommodation in the converted outbuildings, and the horses in the fields beyond.

The sitting room was accessed by a door labelled 'Private', which was a little further along the corridor from the door to Room 7. Like the door of Room 7, the Private door was always locked, and only Philip had the keys. There was a communicating door between the two rooms.

The door that led to the secret room was the back of what to the uninformed observer was a built-in cupboard in the bathroom. Philip had installed the cupboard with its false back after all the workmen had left. There was one other way into the place where he could experience bliss, and that was from the sitting room – a removable panel behind the sideboard allowed access on hands and knees.

A day came when there was a very sticky moment which alarmed Philip greatly. It was late afternoon, and he had come upstairs to Room 7 to have a shower and get changed ready for the evening. He had already decided which cravat to put on, and was whistling happily as he approached the door.

Then Carol had appeared as if from nowhere, and had offered to clean his room! He had nearly lost his poise. He had nearly shouted at her. Just in time he was able to put on his best managerial approach, and had told her that it would not be necessary. After that he ensured that she no longer did any cleaning upstairs. Later he was glad to note that when restricted to the ground floor, the sight of Carol did not affect him adversely any more. Again she merged into the staff machine – a faceless cog.

After nearly eighteen months at *Field Fare*, Carol handed in her notice, and then left. Philip had not expected to feel anything at all, but he was affected by a mixture of conflicting feelings that left him in a state of considerable discomfort. The first feeling was one of profound relief. This puzzled him greatly. After all Carol had been faceless for some time, so why should her permanent absence affect him like this? Before he had time to find an answer to that question, the feeling was joined by one of extreme agitation.

The consequence of these feeling states was that his habitual calm was severely disrupted. He tried his best to conceal this from the staff and the customers, but it took a great deal of energy and concentration to do so, and he began to spend an increasing amount of time alone, staring out of the window of his sitting room from behind his net curtains. His secret room held no attraction for him. Its door remained shut, and instead he would pay visits to the wine cellar at the dead of night, in a desperate search for something that would numb the worst of the feelings.

By great good fortune, the hotel receptionist informed Philip only a few weeks later that she would be leaving quite soon. Apparently she was to move house to be near her daughter, who was expecting a baby. Straight away Philip advertised for a replacement, and this not only provided a welcome diversion, but also brought April into the life of the hotel. April was young, pleasant, and very efficient. Philip was sure that her personality and appearance would complement the attractions of his hotel admirably. She asked for a temporary contract of nine months, and he agreed to this without demur, confident that after

11

this time had elapsed she would be sure to ask for a permanent post. He offered her the use of one of the outbuilding units to live in, and she was clearly pleased to accept.

She started work within the week, and Philip soon forgot the troublesome feelings that he had endured in the wake of Carol's leaving. The state of inner calm that he had previously relied upon returned. There were no more trips to the wine cellar, and he resumed his nightly enjoyment of his secret room. He made one change to it – by placing in the centre of one wall a pleasing painting of flowers that bloomed in the month of April. In the late evenings, Philip would often stand behind the net curtain that cloaked his window, waiting to catch a glimpse of April.

Nine months passed, and then April left to run the office of her boyfriend's garage business. Philip entered a state of profound shock. He went about his work like an automaton, with a fixed smile on his face. He was still aware that he must protect the future of his precious business, and he managed each day by putting more and more energy into it, thus masking his inner state of intense agitation and a crushing feeling of deadness. His staff and guests saw only a man who inspired them with his vast knowledge of food and wine.

One night he made a desperate decision. He screwed the panel from his living room to the secret room firmly into place. Then he filled the bathroom cupboard with a stack of pillows and duvets, thus obscuring any sight of the back of it. The secret room had ceased to exist...

Chapter Five

Philip looked at the calendar. 'Three years,' he murmured. 'We should have a celebration.' The time had passed surprisingly quickly. The business had flourished amazingly well. The end of May had certainly been a good time of year for the Opening – for the first time throwing open the doors of *Field Fare* to the public.

The third anniversary had been last week, but he could organise something for later on. 'Yes, I could do something in September,' he said aloud. 'Three years, three months, three weeks and three days. That's it!' He consulted the calendar again. 'The middle of September... Ideal!'

From then on his mind was full of plans. He called a meeting of all the staff, who showed immediate enthusiasm for the event. They added suggestions of their own, many of which Philip adopted cheerfully.

The days of his extra-busy life rushed by, and there was no time to think of the satin room that he had boarded up and hidden from himself. And yet a resonance of it lingered on in the corners of his mind enough that if he saw a satin lining in a guest's coat, he would find himself fingering it as he hung it in the cloakroom.

The week before the Great Day, Philip woke with a start. Through the tiny window of his spartan single-bedded room he could see the beginnings of a fine day. This was surely a good omen? But something was amiss. He clutched his abdomen and realised that he felt desperately hungry. He glanced at the small clock that stood on his bedside table. It was almost half past six.

He jumped out of bed, grabbed his dressing gown, and ran lightly down the stairs. In the big kitchens he grabbed a small cardboard box, filled it from the fridges with pots of cream and yoghurt, and rushed back to his room. Thank goodness there had been no one about. Staff would soon be stirring, and beginning the early preparations.

Back in bed, he tore the lid off one of the pots of cream and dug his forefinger deep into its slippery contents. Tipping his head back, he allowed the cream to trickle into the back of his mouth. He swallowed it gratefully. Then he repeated the same actions again and again, working through several pots from the box, until at last he felt replete.

Philip relaxed completely. He lay back on his pillow and reflected. He thought of Carol and he thought of April. Then he realised that he *must* have a woman – not just someone whom he could see moving around in his hotel, but a woman who would share his special room.

Philip sat bolt upright. Maybe the forthcoming event would provide an opportunity for him to address this new, and very acute, longing. His mind raced. He would need someone who was planning to stay the night. But each of the five double bedrooms was already booked – by couples. The staff accommodation in the converted outbuildings was hardly likely to attract a lone woman, and in any case it, too, was full.

A slow smile spread across Philip's face as a plan began to form in his mind. Maybe there would be a lone woman at the event… one who had had more to drink than was wise… and who needed a bed for the night. He could offer Room 7. He would make no charge. After all, although adequate, the facilities were quite basic. And then…

Greatly restored, Philip sprang out of bed and embraced the day with remarkable zest and vigour.

The Celebration Day was a resounding success. *Field Fare* was filled with overflowing bowls of autumn fruits, it was decorated with complex straw weaving and corn dollies, and each room had pots of glowing chrysanthemums of copper and yellow hues. Philip had covered a display board with the history of the original farmhouse and the plans of the reconstruction and extensions that had eventually created *Field Fare.* He set this up in the hall.

The guests arrived by car and by taxi. A group arrived by minibus. And of course there were the ten guests who were occupying the five double bedrooms. Everyone gathered in the hall, ready for the start of breakfast, which was a long, slow, delightful affair. The dining room was packed, and tables in the conservatory accommodated a further fifteen people.

The guests were encouraged to spend the rest of the morning on a coach tour round several of the small parish churches in the locality, each of which held fascinating records that could be viewed. Philip had researched this option extensively, and consequently was able to make it especially attractive. He was pleased to note that every guest took it up with enthusiasm. It was important to him to have a little time to himself before lunch, and he knew that he could rely upon the kitchen staff to advance the preparation of that meal without his supervision.

The lunch menu was based on a nutritious soup made from beans and root vegetables. The recipe for this was one of the oldest that Philip had in his collection. The wholemeal brown rolls had pine kernels and celery seeds embedded in them, and the accompanying rich yellow butter had been made at a local farm.

In the middle of the afternoon, guests were encouraged to take a walk through the fields. Leaflets giving directions for several different routes were provided. For those who were less active, Philip provided a range of unusual herbal teas – served in delicate china cups – and the opportunity to look through material he had recently acquired for his farmhouse recipe collection.

It was while these guests were sipping tea that Philip first spied his prey. She was part of a group of older people, and like them was engrossed in studying recipes. This gave him the ideal opportunity to study her. She was dressed in a stunning suit of a coppery-yellow colour. Its simple style and radiant hues were effective in making her stand out. Her fair hair was waved, and was tied back with a ribbon that matched her suit almost exactly. Her handbag was made of wickerwork. On her feet she wore yellow slipperettes.

Philip's mouth watered. He picked up a teapot and made his way across to the group.

'Ladies, could I tempt you to sample some peppermint tea?' he asked.

Several of the group accepted his offer, but the Yellow Lady did not. She was studying a recipe very closely, and gave no sign of having heard him. He was about to repeat his question when he noticed that the ribbon in her hair was made of satin. His hands began to tremble, and the teapot almost slipped out of them. Quickly he gathered himself and took a breath. Before he had a chance to say anything, she reached down to her handbag, put it on her knee, and opened it. Philip could see that the lining was also made of satin. This was too much for him.

'I must replenish this teapot,' he said hurriedly, and retreated to the kitchen to recover.

Calmed by the task of brewing another kind of tea, he returned to the group and offered some to the Yellow Lady.

'Thank you very much,' she replied in a voice that reminded him of the sound of clear water running over pebbles in the bottom of a shallow stream.

'This is made from a mixture of petals and berries,' he explained in a voice which, although not overtly seductive, held some of the same tones and inflections.

She smiled at him. 'Sounds wonderful.'

He concentrated on pouring the sweet smelling liquid into her cup, at the same time scanning her fingers for any sign of a ring. There was one on the middle finger of her right hand. He froze for only a second. Surely that ring was merely for adornment?

She sipped from her cup. 'It's exquisite,' she murmured. She turned to the others and advised seriously, 'You mustn't miss this experience.'

This was followed by instant clamouring for a sample of the brew, and for a while Philip was distracted by the eager demands. The pouring completed, he started to wonder why the Yellow Lady had chosen not to walk that afternoon. She looked as if she were an energetic kind of person. Then he overheard her speaking to one of the others.

'Yes, I would have loved to go across the fields today, but I seem to have pulled something in my foot, and walking is quite painful.'

The other clucked sympathetically, and the Yellow Lady expressed the view that she was sure the pain would settle down soon.

Philip backed away from the group and returned to the kitchens to supervise some of the preparation for the sumptuous dinner that he had planned as the climax of this day. He felt relaxed now, and... complete. The food preparations were more or less second nature to him, and he gave them little conscious thought. His mind was free to plan how he was going to entice this delectable person to stay the night.

During dinner, Philip contrived to hover near to the Yellow Lady's table as often as he possibly could. He had hoped that she would have been at a table in the conservatory, where the setting was slightly more intimate, but he was disappointed. However, instead, he circulated round all the tables in the dining room, endeavouring to steer near to hers as frequently as seemed plausible. He plied her with a mellow wine while she was eating pigeon, but she declined his offers with a sweet smile.

It was later that he saw his chance. He overheard her ordering trifle. He intercepted her dish, and poured a liberal quantity of best cherry brandy on to the trifle.

By now it was getting late, and taxis were arriving for many of the guests. The Yellow Lady seemed to be in no hurry, savouring each mouthful of the trifle. He watched her carefully. Her companions left, and she began to look very tired. There were only a few people left in the dining room, and they were preparing to leave. He moved swiftly to her side.

'Can I call you a taxi?' he enquired politely.

'Er… I have my own transport, thank you,' she replied. 'This trifle is excellent,' she commented, taking another mouthful.

'Would you like another portion?' he asked, trying hard to conceal his excitement.

'I don't think so. I really should be going. I seem to have taken longer than everyone else.' She put down her spoon and tried to stand, but she was unsteady, and her painful foot nearly gave way.

Philip grabbed her elbow, and helped her to sit down again. 'There's no need to hurry,' he assured her. 'We have a considerable amount of clearing up to do before we shut everything down for the night.'

'My head feels rather strange,' she said, putting her hand on her forehead. 'I normally avoid alcohol, but I think that trifle had some in it.'

Philip's excitement increased considerably, but he kept his voice steady when he said, 'Perhaps you would like to lie down for a while. By chance I have a single room available upstairs. It's Room 7.'

'How kind of you. I'd like to do that.'

'I can give you a hand up the stairs,' Philip suggested. He reached out to take her arm, and she accepted his help without any hesitation.

Earlier that day he had disguised the connecting door between the bedroom and his sitting room with a heavy wall hanging, so that its existence was not apparent. He had also moved all the pillows and duvets out of the bathroom cupboard, and although he had left the back in place, it was loose.

It was not long before he was letting her into Room 7, and he sat her on the edge of the bed.

'The bathroom is over there,' he told her as he pointed to it. 'Take your time. And I must assure you that if you decide you want to stay all night, there will be no problem.'

Philip returned nearly an hour later. He hovered briefly in the corridor outside Room 7. Then he slipped through the door marked 'Private', pulled the sideboard away from the low panel and crawled through into the secret room. From there he moved silently through the back of the cupboard in the bathroom, and peered into the bedroom. She was fast asleep, fully clothed, on his single bed.

Success! But then a thought struck him. How would he manoeuvre her into the secret room?

Some time during the evening, he had heard a guest call her by name – Veronica – but he was not interested in that. To him she was the Yellow Lady – the lady with a yellow satin ribbon, yellow satin in her handbag, and yellow satin slipperettes.

He advanced into the room and stood beside the bed, watching her regular breathing. She seemed to exude a faint perfume, which reminded him of the petal and berry tea she had consumed earlier. There was no need to move her. She was here, for him.

After a while he returned to the satin room, leaving the door at the back of the bathroom cupboard open wide. As he lay on the satin-covered bed, he fancied that he could hear the slow rhythm of her breathing.

That night Philip did not sleep. He wanted to savour each moment of this wonderful experience. He felt completely relaxed, and from this state he entered another, infinitely more wonderful, in which he dwelled in complete harmony with himself. The Yellow Lady did not stir.

At six o'clock, he rose and quietly pushed the back door of the bathroom cupboard shut, securing it from his side so that it could not be shifted. Then he crawled through into his sitting room and stood for a while at the window, watching through the net curtains. Later he took clean clothes and a towel to the shower downstairs, which was in the changing room that he had installed specifically for those who had arranged to dine at *Field Fare* after a day's walking.

Seven o'clock saw him in the kitchens preparing a breakfast tray, and at seven thirty precisely, he was in the corridor outside Room 7, tapping on the door. A minute passed, and he was about to tap again when the door opened, and the Yellow Lady was standing there. Her hair was slightly ruffled, but apart from that she looked exactly the same as she had the previous evening.

She drew her breath in slightly, and said, 'Oh! That's so kind of you. You shouldn't have bothered.' She took the tray from him, and added, 'I have some spare clothes in the boot of my car. I'll have a cup of tea, and then I'll go down and get them.'

'If you give me the car key, I can bring them to you,' Philip offered.

'How kind! Are you sure?'

'Of course.'

She disappeared with the tray and returned with her car key.

'It's a metallic grey Ford Focus, a year old.'

Philip took the key. He floated downstairs in a kind of haze, went out of the front door and looked for her car. He opened the boot and found a compact black zip bag, which he took in one hand while he shut the boot with the other. Back in the hotel, he went up the stairs two at a time, and found that she was waiting for him at the door of Room 7.

'I won't be long,' she said apologetically.

'There's no need to rush.'

'But surely the maid will need access quite soon.'

Philip thought quickly. 'The booking for tonight has been cancelled.'

The Yellow Lady glanced at her watch. 'In any case I must be away from here by nine thirty at the latest.'

Philip nodded, and she disappeared inside the room.

As soon as the Yellow Lady had left, Philip rushed to Room 7, shut the door and locked it. Then he flung himself face down on the single bed and took several deep breaths. Perfect! Her essence had lived on, trapped in the bedding.

When at last he stood up again, he began to gather all of it together, intending to move it to the secret room. But then he stopped. *It was the wrong kind of bedding.* He could not have this bedding in his secret room if it was not made of satin!

So great was his conflict that Philip felt as if his heart was being squeezed and twisted. What should he do? He let go of the bundle and rushed into the bathroom. The towels... He could not remember which he had put out the previous day. Were they his favourite ones – the ones with the embroidered satin inset? But alas, they were not. They were the deep pile pair with the velour backing. He touched them, but drew back and shook his head sadly. No, they would not do. Sadness overwhelmed him, and a single tear made its way down his right cheek. He stood there silently in contemplation.

After a while, an idea came to him. Purposefully he went out into the corridor, locking the door behind him. Then he disappeared through the door marked Private, and secured it carefully. Back in the secret room, he took a spare satin sheet from a drawer under the bed, and returned to the Yellow Lady's scent through the back of the bathroom cupboard. Tenderly, he took the bedding and wrapped it carefully in the satin sheet. Then he returned to the secret room and placed it on the bed – exactly where he had spent the night.

Satisfied with this arrangement, he closed both entrances, made sure that the doors marked Private and Room 7 were locked, and returned to his work in the hotel, secure in the knowledge that during those hours her essence was slowly impregnating his satin bed. This awareness engendered in him such a feeling of completeness that the only refreshment he took that day was small sips of coffee – laced with double cream.

Chapter Six

With the undeniable success of his hotel enterprise, Philip had long ago proved to himself that he was a competent businessman, and he knew that he was well respected. The consideration of whether or not there were other aspects of his manhood that might be explored had never come into his conscious mind, but the addition of the essence of the Yellow Lady to his secret room had certainly made him feel that he had grown an inch or two in height. And in addition to that, somehow there was an indefinable shift in the way he experienced the presence of women in their sixties and beyond. When he considered this, he imagined that it must be something to do with his benefactor – the distant relative whose money had made all this possible. Yet there were times when he fancied that there was more to it. These were the women who were long past childbearing years, and instead had other contributions to make.

He did not dwell on the attributes of the Yellow Lady. In any case he already had all he needed from her – the essence.

News of the unique experience of the Celebration Day had spread quickly, and Philip had been inundated with requests to host other celebratory events. However, he turned them all down. All he wanted was the normal well regulated routine of his hotel, without anything to disturb it. His inner energies were concentrated on his experience of the essence of the Yellow Lady, and he did not want to be involved in anything that might distract him. By day he carried the knowledge of it in his core, and by night he revelled in it.

Always polite and courteous, Philip never caused offence when he turned down a request. However, he did find it very difficult when would-be customers persisted, particularly about weddings. He had a strong aversion to such goings-on. Some such people would try to persuade him by offering him an excessive fee, but he was adamant. He had made his decision long ago. *Field Fare* would never host weddings. Those who questioned this were merely told that the hotel was primarily for quiet dining out.

The truth was that Philip hated weddings, and wanted nothing at all to do with them. He found the whole concept deeply disturbing and offensive, and did everything he could to ensure that he rarely, if ever, had to think about them. Fortunately his current receptionist was adept at fending off such requests. However, there were times when not even she could convince the caller that wedding parties were not accommodated at *Field Fare*, and she had to engage him in the unpleasant task of confirming this. Philip often felt drained by such interactions, but since the advent of the Yellow Lady, he found that he was quickly restored by a top-up of her essence in the secret room.

After the Celebration Day, the Christmas and New Year festivities had been something of a chore. Philip put this down to the fact that at the darkest time of the year he would have liked to spend more time in the secret room.

Eventually he remedied the situation by making the decision to close the hotel for several days at the end of January. He had never done such a thing before. Members of staff were amazed and alarmed, and at first rumours went round that he might close the hotel forever. When he heard of this he called everyone together straight away, and reassured them that such a move was so far from his mind that he had been astonished to learn that they had worried about it.

Only two of the live-in staff remained during those precious days, and of course, their accommodation was not within the hotel building itself. Judicious checking from behind the net curtain in his sitting room meant that Philip could see that they left each morning before eight, and returned at eleven at night. These movements coincided with the skeleton bus service that operated along the through road three quarters of a mile away. It was therefore simple to ensure that he encountered neither of them. The odd-job man carried out the essential task of coming to check the central heating boiler every day, but he did not penetrate beyond the basement, since he accessed this through its own external door.

Philip had let everyone believe that he was going away for a few days. After the first night, he had given his mobile phone number to the odd-job man in case of emergency, and he had driven off in his car, having first secured all the doors of the hotel. It was indeed fortunate that he had his own lock-up garage in the hotel grounds, well away from the staff quarters. He arrived back in the middle of the night, hid his car in its garage, and slipped back into the hotel. Before leaving he had taken the precaution of switching off the power to the security light at the side door, so that when he returned he could enter the hotel in darkness.

Alone at last, he was now completely free to discover more of his life in relation to the Yellow Lady!

The first thing he did was to discard all his clothing, and leave it on the spartan single bed. Then he dashed through the bathroom cupboard into the satin room, untied the precious satin parcel, and dived into the essence-impregnated bedding. His chest felt as if it would burst, and the shout of joy that exploded from him was a sound that he had never heard before. For a moment he wondered where it could have come from, but then he made that sound again, and knew then that it was definitely his own. And it was full of colour, strength… and passion!

He rolled on the precious bedding and he slid his body around it – pressing hard into it. He nuzzled it, he nibbled it and he bit it. His mouth filled with saliva and it flowed out in trails. There was a new and wonderful sensation growing in his body. With each movement, the intensity of it grew. It grew and it grew… and it grew.

In this timeless state, the hours of the night flowed by. Philip was completely exhausted by the time the pale winter light showed itself through the high window of his room. He wrapped himself in the black satin robe that he had bought when his room had been completed. He had never worn it before, and he shivered with delight. He slipped his feet into a pair of cork-soled open sandals, and made his way downstairs. The cork felt smooth and warm, and he was not troubled by the fact that there was no satin on it.

In the kitchens, he selected a large double-handled pan made of stainless steel. Then he heated some water, poured it into the pan, and took a sizeable opaque rectangular container out of one of the large refrigerators. The container was clearly labelled in block capitals – DO NOT OPEN. He removed its lid almost reverently and gazed inside. It was filled with cartons of double cream – organically produced. He took out three cartons and placed them in the warmed water.

Once the cream had reached the desired temperature, he took the pan and its treasured contents upstairs. Then he went swiftly to his sideboard, and took out a jar of honey. This was no ordinary honey. It was made from bees that lived and worked in acres of meadows in which grew multiple species of wild flowers.

Back in the secret room, he wrapped himself in the satin sheet that had held inside it the Yellow Lady's bedding, lay on the now-exposed quilt that she had inhabited, and fed himself with finger-drips of honeyed cream. Then he fell asleep.

Philip slept very soundly. He did not wake until all daylight had gone, and when he did, he found himself in exactly the same position he last remembered. He lay there for a long time, in a state of total relaxation and fulfilment.

When at last he stood up, he felt a little unsteady. The feeling was pleasant, and was somehow entwined with a sense of confidence and security. Philip did not question why that should be. He wanted only to enjoy it. He carried the feeling with him to the shower, where he spent a long time revelling in the effect of the warm water cascading down his body. Occasionally he added a few drops of lightly perfumed oil to the experience. Then he leaned against the warmed side panel of the shower with his eyes closed until his legs folded beneath him in a quite delectable way, and he slid to the bottom of the shower cabinet, where he was content to sit for a while.

At length he enveloped himself in a large towel and returned to the satin bed. Until now it had been unthinkable to allow the spartan bedding to meet with the satin bedding, except when wrapped up in a satin sheet. Yet now he could see that the spartan bedding had tangled with the satin bedding, and from what he remembered of the night, this had taken place in a kind of merging ceremony that he had conducted. He climbed into the muddle and fell asleep again.

When he woke he felt refreshed. He had no idea of the time, and had no wish to know. His energies restored, he was ready to revel in his newfound occupation again, and once more he unleashed his body in the bed – to express itself and evolve into its true state.

That night was even more satisfying than the one before. Philip was on a voyage of discovery, and the treasures he was unearthing were beyond price. The cream and honey feeds became more frequent, and somehow more exciting, and he had a growing sense that they were energising him towards something that was pivotal.

Philip was enormously glad of the short gloomy days. At this very special time, his ideal would have been to have continuous night.

It was during the third night that the most wondrous thing took place. Revelling ever more confidently in the tumble of bedding, his spirit flying free, Philip became aware of another new sensation. He had at first thought it was more of the explosive feeling that culminated in his joyful shouts, but as it became more prominent, he knew that it was not. His passion heightened, and he thrust his head strongly into the disarray of bedding. At that moment his mind filled with the image of a stag – huge, mighty and glorious. He burrowed his imaginary antlers into the bedding and tossed it around, laughing in a way he had not known before.

And then it happened. An unimaginable explosion – but entirely real. Bliss... Ecstasy... He seemed somehow to be suspended, floating. And then there was ultimate peace.

He slept again, for a long time.

When he opened his eyes, Philip knew several things. The first was that he had undergone a transformation. Nothing would ever be the same again.

Yet soon he would have to get up and go about his daily business. He pondered this necessity. The first thing to do would be to check the date and the time.

He took a quick shower, and dressed in clean everyday clothes. Then he switched the radio on in his living room. Reassured by the discovery that he had nearly twenty-four hours left to himself before his staff returned to resume work, he sat down to contemplate his situation.

Realising that he was ravenously hungry, he decided to concentrate on cooking something satisfying. He was astonished to discover that his mind filled with images of roast venison, and he went straight to the kitchen to begin preparations. Gone were his former preferences of scrambled eggs, puréed soups and delicately flavoured custards.

That day he feasted on game for breakfast, lunch and supper, with snacks of game in between. Sinking his teeth into the tender flesh was an exquisite sensation. The feeling that animal blood was merging with his own brought him to a state of hyper-excitement, and he spent some time looking through his sitting room window with high-powered binoculars, scanning the fields for game birds.

At times, Philip mused about redesigning his private rooms.

27

His spartan single room could be revamped into an attractive space for sharing. Its modest proportions would not be constrained if he installed a comfortable three-quarter bed. The sitting room would need a good carpet, a fireplace with a real flame gas fire, full length lined curtains of high quality, and a sumptuous sofa. A slow smile spread across his face as he promised himself that he would find one where the back would let down to make a substantial upholstered plinth. The ugly sideboard must be chopped up, and the low entrance to the secret room could be concealed by a new, well-stocked drinks cabinet.

By the end of the day, Philip had cleared up in the secret room. He would dispose discretely of the tangle of used bedding. Using a duvet from the hotel, he would sleep on the bed that night, but afterwards he would close up the secret room and begin the process of furnishing his other rooms to a high standard. There would be no need for secrecy about this. Staff would not think it remarkable. In fact, replacement of his furniture could be considered long overdue, as his business had clearly been thriving for a long time.

Chapter Seven

Those who noticed a change in Philip put it down to the fact that he had gained obvious benefit from a well-earned holiday. In any case, the change was not immediately striking. It was more that there was a small shift in many aspects of his personality, and these were not all apparent at the same time.

Those who helped him to put his new furniture in place and remove the old merely wondered why he had not had this quality of décor installed earlier.

As Philip went about his work, more and more he identified himself as a hunter, stalking. He fantasised about how he would entrap his prey, and what he would do with it. In the privacy of his rooms, he made an ever-expanding list of possible scenarios.

Perhaps he could offer a monthly draw, and ensure that the winner was a suitable female. Of course, the prize would be a free dinner followed by a free night in Room 7 – to be used some time that month. Maybe there could be an event that allowed customers to take a special interest in the operation of the kitchens. A guided tour followed by an intimate drink in the room marked 'Private' would ensure further pleasures. Female occupants of the staff quarters could be invited for an evening's entertainment. Likewise, particularly interesting single ladies who were dining might be enticed... And there was always the possibility of a traveller who had lost her way.

As the list extended, Philip thought of a sensational possibility! Maybe he could after all offer a wedding party at *Field Fare*. Then he could arrange to put the groom out of action for the night, and steal the bride. This was a plan that greatly commended itself to him. Now that he had undergone his transformation, surely such an endeavour would be the pinnacle of his achievements?

There was no hurry. Each engagement must be planned carefully, and he was certain that the planning would be almost as fulfilling as the event itself.

Chapter Eight

Carrie was nineteen. She had worked at *Field Fare* for nearly a year. She had started as a part-time cleaner, but had been encouraged to learn other skills, and was now competent in the kitchens and as a waitress, progressing to being a full-time employee. Over the past three months she had lived in one of the units that had been made from the farm outbuildings. She liked Mr Thornton because he was always the same. Her own father was quite unpredictable, and she usually felt on edge around him. Here at *Field Fare* she had begun to relax, and as a result her competence had revealed itself. She was a hard worker, intelligent and enthusiastic.

Carrie had spent the January days off at home, and she had enjoyed her time there very much. She had been surprised to find that she was far less disturbed by her father's behaviour, and for the first time they had some pleasant conversations. If he tried to steer the interaction into something she didn't like, she was able to ensure that it soon returned to something of mutual interest. The confidence she had developed at work was certainly benefiting her at home. Her mother, who was normally a quiet woman, noticed the change, and warmed to the new situation.

Carrie was short and dumpy. Her cheeks were habitually a healthy red colour. She did not wear make-up. Her brown hair was thick and quite long, and she liked to use a variety of clasps to secure it in one or another of several ingenious arrangements that she devised. Her secret desire was to become a hairdresser, and she was saving up to pay for an initial training course.

Philip made his decision. He would do some practising, and he felt that the maid-of-all-work who had been at the hotel for about a year would be ideal for the purpose. Living just across the back yard meant that she was easily accessible. Now, what was her name? He always referred to such females in his mind as Dolly, but he didn't think that was her name. He had noticed that the upward tilt to her small nose was quite attractive. At least it meant that her nose wouldn't get in the way of anything.

That evening Carrie was working as a waitress in the packed dining room. Philip watched her closely as he moved around the guests, entertaining them with cravat tales and other interesting information. He could see that she had just the right balance of warmth and professionalism. He had certainly chosen well when he had drawn her into the life of the hotel.

Now he contrived that their paths crossed. As she was taking a tray of used plates away, he took two brisk steps backwards and they collided.

'I'm so sorry, Mr Thornton!' she exclaimed in a low voice.

Philip was greatly impressed by the way she had saved the plates from crashing to the floor. 'It was an accident,' he reassured her. He patted her back, allowed his fingers to linger for an extra second or two, and then moved to another table.

Later than evening, he intercepted her as she left to cross the yard.

'You did very well,' he told her. 'Can I treat you to a nightcap?'

'No, thank you,' she replied. 'I don't take such things.'

She took a few steps forward, but he strode ahead and then stood in front of her.

'Some of my cordial?'

Carrie was tempted. Mr Thornton's cordial, made from a secret recipe, was highly sought after, and it would be a great treat to have even a sip of it. She hesitated, and Philip seized the moment.

'I have to see to something, but if you come and knock on my door in about ten minutes, I'll give you a glass of it.'

Carrie was uncertain. 'I…'

'I won't keep you up,' Philip promised.

That seemed to settle Carrie, and she agreed. 'It's the door marked Private, isn't it?' she asked.

'That's correct.' Philip turned and walked briskly back into the hotel. Once inside, he ran upstairs, poured the drink, and waited. The cordial required dilution, but he had deliberately chosen to ignore this.

Ten minutes later, there was a tap at the door. Philip opened it and invited her in, shutting the door behind her. He noticed that she looked a little nervous.

'You must be tired,' he commented. He pointed to the large sofa. 'Do sit down. I'll pour you some cordial, and soon you'll be settling down for the night.'

He took the drink from the cabinet, handed it to her, and watched while she sipped it.

'It's just like they say,' she told him. 'It's wonderful.'

'I'm glad you're enjoying it,' he replied. 'You deserve it.'

He watched while she finished it and then began to loll against the back of the sofa. Gently he flattened it until she was lying down, unconscious. The concoction had done its work, and now, in this close proximity to her, he could express himself fully.

The following morning, Carrie woke with a start. At first she had no idea where she was. The ceiling looked unfamiliar, and her head felt muzzy. She tried to move, but her arms and legs felt leaden. She was quite thirsty, and looked around to see if she could get some water. Then she gasped as she realised where she was.

Philip had been checking on her condition by watching from his bedroom through a concealed peephole. Now she was awake, he went out into the corridor, locked the door of Room 7, and opened the Private door.

Carrie was very embarrassed.

'I'm so sorry, Mr Thornton. I can't imagine what happened.' She tried to stand up, but her legs were unsteady.

'You must have been sickening for something,' Philip said

sympathetically. 'You fell asleep as soon as you finished your drink. Let me help you to your room, and you can rest there until you feel better.'

Carrie was greatly relieved. Mr Thornton was being kind and understanding, and there was no hint that she had jeopardised her job.

As they went through the kitchens towards the yard, Philip remarked to a passing member of staff, 'She doesn't seem very well today. I'll take her to her room, and she can lie down for a while.'

Relaxing on her own bed, Carrie took stock of her situation. She was only rarely unwell, and this state had come on very quickly. She didn't remember falling asleep, so she surmised that she must have more or less passed out. What must Mr Thornton have thought of her? And there was something else… but she couldn't quite put her finger on it. Feeling very weary, she began to doze.

When she came to again, several hours had passed, and she was glad to find that she felt much better. She went for a shower and put on clean clothes. It wouldn't be long before dinner was served. If she went to the kitchens and made something simple that she could eat, she should be ready in time to do her waitressing.

As she crossed the yard, she was relieved to find that she felt stable. Everyone in the kitchen was hard at work, and paid little attention to her, although someone did remark that it was good to see her looking well again.

As she took the first of the starters into the dining room, she was surprised when Mr Thornton shot her a rather strange glance. She concentrated on serving the guests, and when she looked in his direction again, he smiled across to her in an encouraging way. Surely she must have been mistaken by her first impression of his attitude towards her? But the memory lingered on, and it joined up with the feeling that there had been something else about the illness that had come on so suddenly in the room marked Private. She thrust these thoughts to one side, as the evening's work was the priority, and she went about her duties pleasantly and efficiently.

The next day Mr Thornton called her into his office, where he invited her to sit down. Then he began to ask some questions.

'An intelligent young woman like you must have plans for a career,' he stated. 'Is your main interest in hospitality, or does it lie elsewhere?'

Carrie was taken by surprise, and answered honestly. 'I like my work very much, but my ambition is to become a hairdresser. I want to work hard here so that I can save up enough money to pay for a course that will give me a start.'

Philip was very glad to hear this. The way was now clear, and soon he would be rid of her.

'Ah, I would never have guessed,' he mused aloud. Turning to Carrie he asked, 'When does the next course begin?'

'Straight after Easter, but I won't have quite enough saved up by then. I was hoping to start after the summer.'

'I might have some extra hours I could offer you,' Philip suggested, almost to himself.

Carrie sat quietly, almost holding her breath.

'At the moment you don't work at weekends. It would be great help if you did six to ten on Saturday evenings until Easter, including Easter weekend. You'll be paid time and a half.'

Carrie's face shone. 'Thank you, Mr Thornton. I'll certainly do that, and I'll put my name down for the course as soon as I can.'

'Off you go now.'

Carrie jumped up and almost skipped out of the room, leaving Philip greatly relieved. Since the night she had spent on his sofa he had felt very uncomfortable in her presence. He was very pleased with how the conversation had gone. In only eight weeks' time she would leave, and he could forget all about her.

There was nothing that could spoil Carrie's happiness. She would begin to study hairdressing a lot sooner than she had anticipated. She told herself that the evasive thing that niggled

35

away at the back of her mind was of no consequence, and she ignored it.

Chapter Nine

Philip found that the weeks passed quite pleasantly. He looked forward to Easter, when lambs would be in the fields, and the days would be lengthening. The presence of Carrie was not a burden to him. In fact he barely noticed her, and apart from an occasional acknowledgement of her presence, he rarely thought about her. Carrie herself was full of excitement about her future, and although she continued to do her work thoroughly, a large part of her mind was occupied with the creation of extravagant hairstyles.

Carrie's last shift was unremarkable. She had already said goodbye to many of the staff, and she had packed up her things that morning. A friend was coming to collect her. Philip watched through his sitting room window as she crossed the yard with her possessions – leaving space for someone else.

He sat up late that night, musing about his next venture. On the whole, what had happened with Carrie had been satisfactory. He allowed his mind to go back to how he had arranged that she spent a night in this room. Yes, it had all gone quite smoothly. And afterwards he had been efficient in organising how to dispose of her in a tidy way, without any unwelcome disturbance. He rubbed his hands together, and his mouth felt quite wet as he contemplated an encounter with someone new.

It was late July, and Elaine was on her way south to Liverpool to see her boyfriend, but had decided to break her journey by spending some time with her Aunt Catherine. Catherine was actually a great-aunt, her maternal grandmother's sister. She lived on her own in a semi-detached cottage in the depths of the Cheshire countryside. Elaine had only been there once before – when she was a child – and had little memory of the exact location, but had brought with her a good map and detailed directions that she had written in a notebook.

She felt annoyed when she took a wrong turning, and found herself driving down a lane that was clearly going nowhere. She was about to stop her car and turn round, when in the failing light she glimpsed a substantial building a little further along the road. She decided to drive on, thinking that she might be able to ask for confirmation of exactly where she was.

The building turned out to be a smallish hotel, named *Field Fare*. 'What an interesting name,' she said aloud as she drew up in the car park. Then she noticed a man inspecting a window box near the front door, and went to speak to him.

'Excuse me,' she began.

The man turned and smiled. Elaine could see that he was well dressed, and that he wore a cravat with an unusual pattern on it.

She continued. 'I've taken a wrong turning, and I wanted to check my list of directions.'

'Why not come inside?' the man invited, gesturing towards the entrance door.

Elaine noticed that the sound of his voice was warm and that he had a cultured accent, although she could not place where it was from.

'Thank you,' she replied. She went inside, and found herself in a pleasant hall, with comfortable chairs positioned around the sides of it.

He held out his hand. 'I'm Philip Thornton.'

Elaine shook it saying, 'I'm Elaine Grant.' She noticed that his handshake felt open and welcoming.

'Please do sit down, and I'll do my best to help,' said Philip. This woman was certainly an attractive proposition. Perhaps he could persuade her to spend the night in Room 7.

Elaine took her map and list of directions out of her bag, and Philip carefully behaved exactly as if he were studying them with her.

'I can see where you went wrong,' he told her. 'It'll take

38

you another forty-five minutes or so to get to your destination.'

'Oh dear,' said Elaine unguardedly, 'I don't particularly like driving in the dark.'

Philip was sympathetic. 'That's not surprising, and bends in the lanes round here can be quite treacherous.' His presentation of himself remained warm and apparently neutral, but inwardly he was rubbing his hands together gleefully. The situation was already looking promising.

However, Elaine surprised him by saying, 'Never mind, I've had plenty of practice, and I'm sure I'll manage. I'd be grateful if you could point me in the right direction, and I'll get on my way.'

Philip could see no other way of proceeding. He gave her the help that she needed, and then went with her to the door, feeling very disappointed. He was about to bid her goodbye, when on impulse he decided to walk with her to her car. It was there he noticed to his great delight that the front nearside tyre was almost completely flat.

'I'm afraid you've got a problem here,' he commented, carefully concealing his excitement.

Elaine was annoyed. 'Oh, no! I have a good spare with me, but trying to change the wheel in the dark with the wrong kind of clothes on really doesn't appeal to me.' She thought for a moment, and then said, 'I think I'll just phone the breakdown service.'

'It might take an hour or so before they arrive,' Philip remarked, trying not to sound pleased.

'Drat! You're absolutely right. I'll have to give my aunt a ring and let her know that I could be quite late.'

'There's another option,' Philip said in a matter-of-fact voice.

Elaine looked at him and waited.

'You could spend the night here.'

Elaine was about to say something, but Philip went on.

'I happen to have a spare room for tonight. It's quite modest accommodation – number 7.' He paused only for a second before adding, 'The odd-job man will be here in the morning, and I can get him to change the wheel for you.'

'I must say I'm tempted to take you up on your offer,' Elaine replied. She took her mobile phone out of her bag. 'I'll have to make a couple of quick calls first.'

Philip smiled. 'Of course.'

He turned and went back into the hotel. It looked as if things were going to turn out to be in his favour after all. The receptionist had by now gone home, and he hovered near the desk, waiting.

A few minutes went by, and then Elaine appeared at the door. She caught sight of him and approached. Philip could feel his heart beating faster. Already he could imagine a delightful scene in Room 7.

'That's it fixed,' Elaine told him. 'I'd like to go ahead and book that room for the night.'

'Can I take your details?' he enquired politely. He entered the information into the computer, and then asked, 'Would you like something to eat?'

Elaine looked uncertain. 'It's rather late.'

'Something light could be brought to your room,' Philip offered.

'That sounds ideal,' she conceded. 'I'd like a sandwich and a bottle of sparkling water, please.'

'And you can have a glass of our special cordial on the house.'

'That sounds nice. Thanks very much. What's it made from?'

Philip smiled. 'I don't divulge that. It's a speciality here.'

Elaine nodded. 'I understand.'

Having shown her to Room 7, Philip went downstairs and looked into the dining room. The lateness of the hour meant that no one was left there. He went into the kitchen, where the last of the clearing up was under way, directed someone to take water and a sandwich to Room 7, and then said that he was retiring for the night.

Once in his sitting room, he allowed time for the woman's supper to be delivered before pouring a generous amount of cordial into a glass. Then he walked briskly to the door of Room 7. She responded promptly to his knock, and seemed very pleased to see what he had brought.

'Oh, thanks!' she said. 'That's really kind of you.'

Philip's voice was almost a purr. 'It's no trouble. I hope you enjoy it and that you have a good night. Although the odd-job man starts work at eight in the morning, you don't need to rush because he'll be here until about one o'clock.'

He walked away at a leisurely pace down the corridor towards the main staircase until he heard the door shut. Then he turned and made his way rapidly to the door marked Private. Once inside his sitting room he pressed his right eye to the peephole.

He was in a state of heightened awareness as he observed that she had tossed her brown slip-on shoes into one corner of the room and was lying on the bed. He wasn't sure whether she had her eyes shut or not. Maybe she was gazing at the ceiling. But in any case that did not matter. A tray was clearly visible on the bedside table. She had consumed all but the crusts of the sandwich. Next to a tumbler, the bottle of sparkling water was half empty, and beside it stood the glass of cordial.

Then she stirred and sat upright, her legs dangling off the bed. She reached for the glass and took a small sip from it. She held the misty amber liquid in her mouth for a few seconds before swallowing it, and the light from the bedside lamp revealed the expression on her face to be one of surprise and pleasure.

Perfect! Everything was going according to plan.

Barely breathing, Philip waited, counting each sip. After the third one, she put the glass down, and began to undress. Her movements were unhurried, and he savoured every one of them. Naked, she pulled a thin nightdress from her overnight bag, and slipped it on over her head. The effect of this on Philip was even greater, and he found it very difficult to contain himself.

She poured more of the water into the tumbler, and drank it all. Then she disappeared into the bathroom, and when she came back she got into bed and switched off the light.

Philip was shocked. What was happening? His intentions had been thwarted. How could she do this to him? Room 7 was in complete darkness. He could no longer see her. He wanted to rip open the connecting door, grab the remaining cordial and pour it down her throat. Then she would be his.

But a distant voice restrained him. He glanced round his room, and then looked out of the window. There was no one to be seen. He threw the door of his room open and looked up and down the corridor. No sign of anyone at all. He shut the door again, and strode over to the peephole. Only blackness met his gaze. His trembling hands hovered over the handle of the connecting door. The voice became louder and more insistent, and it was only then that he realised it was coming from *inside* his head. His hands dropped to his sides, and he went to the sofa and collapsed on to it.

Seconds later he was filled with rage. How dare she? He leapt to his feet and stormed round the room in a frenzy that soon turned to fury. He wanted to smash something. If only he could go into Room 7, he would throw away the last of her sparkling water, and he would rip her clothes to shreds.

His whole body juddered with the effort of preventing himself from taking such action, which if followed through would expose his secret life. It was paramount that it should be protected from any possible harm. But what could he do with his feelings? Revenge. That was it! He must devise a plan straight away. Yet he knew that acting out revenge would lead to the destruction of something that was pivotal to his very existence, and again he collapsed helplessly on to his sofa.

Then the answer came to him. Clearly he had made a stupid mistake. She was horrible, and could never have fulfilled the role that he had imagined. This realisation gave him some relief, and he began to relax.

Yet this state was only short-lived. He was now filled with

such a yearning that he had to hide his face in a large cushion to mute a howl that came from deep inside, and he felt as if he was drowning in a feeling akin to intense grief. Lying on the sofa with the cushion wrapped round his face, his body racked with sobs, wailing seemed to emanate from the depths of his soul. And yet there was no sound.

When Philip woke, he felt stiff. For a moment he wondered why he was still fully clothed, but then the events of the previous evening flooded back into his mind. The dampness of the cushion near his face confirmed his memories. He was glad to note that apart from feeling uncomfortable, he was otherwise unaffected. After all, he told himself, the point of all this was to gain experience, and that's what had happened last night. Conveniently, he had woken before the early staff began work, and he went downstairs to the shower to get washed, shaved and changed.

Back in his sitting room, he checked the peephole. There was no change. All was still in darkness. It was now half past six. He decided to collect his breakfast from the kitchens, and then go to his office and work there. If she had not appeared by nine, he would send one of the female staff to knock on her door and offer a tray of something.

By nine, Philip had cleared his desk. Satisfied with his progress, he went to find someone to waken that woman. What was her name? He couldn't remember it. He checked the computer at reception. Ah yes... Ms Elaine Grant. Having sent Tricia, the temporary chambermaid, on the errand, he settled himself back at his desk, and began to sort through a file of papers.

Ten minutes later, Tricia tapped on the door of his office.

'What is it?' he asked amiably.

'I tried several times, but I can't get an answer,' Tricia replied.

'Try again in half an hour.'

Philip felt a little puzzled, but turned back to his work, and

43

quickly became sufficiently involved in it that he jumped when he heard a knock on the door and Tricia reappeared.

'Try again at ten,' he instructed.

After this he could not settle to his work. He went up to his sitting room, and looked through the peephole. The weak daylight that crept round the curtains was enough to show that the woman was still in bed, and was not moving. Philip began to feel uneasy. She should be awake by now. He fixed his eye to the hole again, and this time he concentrated on the tray beside her bed. He could just make out that both the tumbler and the glass were empty.

Philip's mind whirled. There was no way of knowing when she had finished the cordial. He already knew that a relative was expecting her later today. If she had drunk the rest of the cordial this morning, she might not stir until the afternoon. What should he do? The most obvious thing would be to get the wheel changed on her car so that she could leave as soon as she was able, but for that he would need to have her key.

He waited in his room until nearly ten, and then went to the top of the stairs, where he did not have to wait long before Tricia appeared. He handed her a key from his pocket.

'This is for Room 7,' he told her without further explanation.

Tricia took it and waited.

Philip went on. 'Ms Grant's car has a flat tyre. She knows about that. If I could have her car key, I could get Joe to change the wheel now. Would you put your head round the door of her room, and if she stirs, ask for the key?'

Tricia knocked on the outer door quite loudly. There was no response, so she opened it with Philip's key, and knocked again on the inner door. Still hearing no reply, she pushed it open and looked inside. She had never been in this room before. In the half light she could see a small double bed with a motionless form in it, and a tray on the bedside table with empty glasses and some crusts on a plate.

'Ms Grant,' she said softly.

The form did not stir.

'Ms Grant,' she repeated, this time more loudly.

Still the form did not stir, so she retreated back into the corridor.

'I can't raise her,' she reported.

'Better leave her to sleep on,' Philip decided. 'I believe she had a stressful journey yesterday. She must be exhausted. I'll have a word with Joe later. Come and try her again in an hour or so.'

When Tricia had gone, Philip returned to his sitting room. This simply wouldn't do. He had had enough. He had to get her out.

In the kitchens he made up a flask of strong coffee. Then he went back to his sitting room, opened the connecting door, and pushed the wall hanging aside. He could hear the sound of her breathing. It was deep and regular. Making no noise, he slipped into the room and poured some coffee into the lid of the flask and placed it on the tray by the bed. Then he returned to his room, repositioned the wall hanging and closed the connecting door. After that he banged on it very loudly several times before checking for any change by peering through the peephole. He repeated this exercise until she began to stir. She moaned a little, and then sat up and hung her legs over the side of the bed, leaning forward and holding her head in her hands. Philip quickly went out into the corridor, locking the door marked Private behind him.

He went to look for Tricia, and found her changing the bed in Room 1.

'You need not return to Room 7 after all,' he told her. 'The guest is up and about.'

'I'm glad to hear that, Mr Thornton,' Tricia replied, hardly looking away from her task. 'There's plenty to get on with.' Then she fumbled in her pocket and produced the room key, which she handed to him. After he had gone, she muttered, 'I can't stand these lay-a-beds.'

Back at the peephole, Philip watched as Elaine drank the

coffee. She had drawn the curtains, and he could see that she looked quite pale. She must have been to the bathroom as she had a face flannel in her hand, which she kept placing across her forehead.

Eventually she disappeared through the door into the bathroom, where he imagined she must be taking a shower, and when she reappeared she moved in a more ordinary way. He watched as she dressed. Then she gathered her things together, opened the window, took several gulps of fresh air, took a last look round and moved towards the door.

Philip waited a good ten minutes before he left his sitting room. Downstairs, he found her seated on one of the chairs in the hall. She was still a little pale, but otherwise seemed normal.

He approached her. 'Did you sleep well?'

'Like a log,' she replied with a wry smile. 'I've phoned my aunt to let her know that I'll be even later than I thought. Is your offer of help from your odd-job man still available?'

'Certainly. I'll go and fetch him.'

Philip soon found Joe, and was back in only a few minutes. The quicker he could get rid of this woman the better. He offered her a light breakfast while Joe was working on her car. He noticed that her face took on a paler shade for a moment, and she declined, saying that she did not feel hungry at this time of day.

The wheel changed, Philip saw her to her car.

'Thanks for everything,' she said as she fastened her seatbelt. 'I'll certainly recommend your services to anyone who might pass this way.'

Clutching the key to Room 7 in his pocket, Philip put on his best smile, at the same time vowing to himself that he would never risk using the cordial again. Until recently he had never used it at this concentration before. The concoction that he had given to that girl he got rid of to the hairdressing course, and now this one, had been many times stronger than the version that he served in the dining room as an after-dinner speciality. No one had ever managed to prise the list of ingredients from

46

him, and he would never divulge it, as it contained small quantities of certain plant extracts that he was a bit unsure about.

From now on his approach would have to be different. The next one would have to know him and willingly agree to be part of his pleasures. He had gathered experience – some good, and some not so good. Now was the time when he must begin to take action that was more direct.

Chapter Ten

The summer weather was warm and pleasant, and all in all, Philip felt quite content as he deliberated on the subject of exactly how to go about netting his next catch. His earlier idea of a prize draw certainly appealed to him. The winner would get the chance of a free night in Room 7, with 'surprise extras'. Yes, that was a good plan. He would draw up an advertisement soon.

After he had made this decision, the staff began to notice that Philip had an especially relaxed smile. As an employer, they nearly always found him to be amiable, and they were glad to see him enjoying the days even more than usual.

Philip decided that he would have a 'Ladies' Night' in about six weeks' time – the second half of September. He would print some flyers and leave them on a side table in the hall, and word would be sure to get round. He would arrange that all bookings should be made only through himself, and that the dining room that evening would be available only to single ladies who were non-residents. On that date, residents' dinners could be accommodated in the conservatory.

He would savour every moment of the preparation for this event, and the climax would be his next intimate adventure. Philip was sure that those six weeks would pass quite quickly, but as the days went by the thought of having to wait so long began to feel burdensome. He began to think that perhaps it would be sensible to have an interim plan.

While designing the flyers for the Ladies' event, he let his mind sift through all the people he already knew – staff, local residents and those who passed through quite regularly. It was when he was contemplating the latter category that he fixed on one woman in particular. Although her name evaded him, he remembered her well. She stayed for a night every few weeks. As far as he was aware, she was someone who travelled up and down the country for the firm which employed her. He liked the fact that she always wore a tailored skirt with a jacket to go with it, and her tights were of great interest to him. That part of her attire was never ostentatious and never plain, and this appealed to him greatly. She always took a keen interest in his cravat of the evening, and he had had to restrain himself from asking about her tights of the day. He imagined that she must be in her late thirties, as the skin in the corners of her eyes took time to spread out after she had crinkled it in a smile. Other than that she showed no signs of ageing. Her hair was a mass of blonde curls, and her figure was beautifully proportioned. Her personality was confident, warm and bubbly, and he was always delighted by the fact that she kept her nails well trimmed. Amanda Adams. Yes, that was her name.

Philip decided to look back through the records to see when she last spent a night at *Field Fare.* He soon located the entry. It was a little over two weeks ago, so maybe it wouldn't be long before she made contact again. He glanced down the bookings for the next few days, but did not see her name. If he remembered correctly, she invariably made contact by e-mail, so it would be easy enough for him to keep an eye open for the next one. Having thought thus far, Philip again focused his energies on planning for the Ladies' event. Soon the flyers would be ready to display in the hall.

It was exactly a week later that Philip spotted the e-mail from AA. She wanted to book in for Wednesday night – only two days away. He replied immediately, letting her know that although the usual rooms were fully booked, he could let her use Room 7, and that she should ask for him personally when she arrived.

It was late on Wednesday afternoon, and nearly time for AA to arrive. Philip carefully selected his most interesting cravat – the mauve one with the embroidered *fleur de lys* design in gold thread. Then he hovered around in the hall, trying to appear as if he were engaged in a number of small tasks. From time to time he popped outside the front door to enjoy the balmy air of late August, and at the same time he looked up the drive, hoping to see her arriving.

At almost seven thirty precisely, a car drew up that he was certain was hers. And he was not disappointed. The car backed into a space not far from the door, and the driver got out. He noted how she swivelled herself round so that both legs protruded from the car almost simultaneously. Her elegantly cut black skirt ended above her knees, and her tights were... fantastic. They were a very pale shade of grey, with some kind of pattern on, but he could not see exactly what that was unless he closed in on her – an action which he felt he should avoid at the moment.

Standing by her car, she opened the rear door and rummaged around, soon pulling out a neat black case on wheels and also a matching handbag.

Philip was beside her in a trice.

'Can I help you?' he asked in silky tones.

She jumped slightly, and turned. When she saw him, she said, 'Oh, thank you' and passed the case to him. At the front door Philip took her elbow as she went up the step and into the hall. He booked her in, and then showed her to Room 7.

'I'll see you in the dining room,' he told her as he left.

Amanda had always enjoyed staying overnight at *Field Fare*. Its informal and intimate atmosphere suited her needs well. She washed, and quickly changed into a simple black cocktail dress, discarding the flat black lace-up shoes she used for driving, and putting on a pair of black high heels. There was no need to change her tights. She completed her outfit by putting a silver chain round her neck that carried an oval pendant, which her father had given her not long before he died. The design on the pendant depicted a leaping dolphin – as a reminder of a wonderful trip that they had shared to see some of these creatures.

Amanda felt relaxed in Mr Thornton's company. She usually engaged in a light conversation with him at some time during each stay. On reflection she realised that there were a number of things about him that reminded her of her father – for example, his accent was almost identical.

She made her way down to the dining room unhurriedly, and was surprised to see Mr Thornton waiting nearby to take her to her table – a small table, set for one, and positioned in a corner near the window. Amanda found that evening to be an absolute delight. Mr Thornton made regular visits to ask how she was enjoying her meal, and each time they would exchange a comment about the natural history of the locality.

Table by table, the diners finished and left. Amanda stayed on, alternately reading her newspaper and responding to Philip's intermittent attentions. When it was time for the dining room to close, he asked if she would like to share a drink with him in his office, where he could show her some of the old records of wildlife that he had gathered together over the years of owning *Field Fare*. Eager to see those papers, Amanda agreed, and soon she was seated in his office, poring over the fascinating material.

Philip edged his chair nearer to hers. The fact that it was an office chair with castors facilitated this manoeuvre, and he was able to contrive that his left knee was positioned so that it touched her right one. Thus gently joined, he leaned towards the document that she was reading as if to share her interest in it.

'This is absolutely fascinating,' she said excitedly. 'It's quite right that your hotel is called *Field Fare*, since breeding pairs of fieldfares used to be common around here.'

'I chose the name myself,' Philip informed her proudly.

Amanda looked at him. 'Did you really? How very clever of you.' She hesitated and then said, 'Perhaps you already knew about the bird life in years gone by.'

'The name came into my head long before I did any research of that kind,' Philip assured her.

'It must have been your instinct,' Amanda concluded.

'I'm inclined to agree.' Philip knew very well that the instinct he was thinking of at that moment was nothing to do with bird populations of the past, and he had no wish to explain otherwise.

He leaned further over the document, as if to study it in more precise detail, and at the same time, he slipped an arm behind her, his hand clasping part of the chair, as if to steady himself. This did not provoke any reaction from her, so he remained in that position – his knee now pressing firmly into hers.

'I've finished reading through that now,' said Amanda. 'Do you mind if I look at the next section?'

'Read at your own pace,' Philip encouraged. 'If necessary I can catch up some other time.'

Amanda read in silence, completely immersed in the material. Philip pretended to be equally absorbed, but in reality he was calculating when and how to continue with his encroachment.

His next step was to move his hand from the chair, trying to avoid losing the contact that his arm had with her back. Carefully he managed to tuck his hand under the periphery of her gluteal muscles. Although she made no sign that she had noted this, it must have impacted on her, as she wriggled backwards an inch or two, so that his hand was more firmly installed in its new position. Philip pondered about whether or not this had been a conscious decision on her part, or if it was merely a kind of settling in, as a cat does when making itself comfortable.

By now the hotel was completely quiet. Philip began to relax, and his body surged with delightful emotions and sensations. Apparently unaware of what was happening, Amanda continued her studies.

As time passed, Philip became more and more aware that he would have to move. For one thing, he was becoming uncomfortable holding this position, and for another, he needed to pay a visit to the bathroom. He was not keen to disrupt the progress that he had made, but it had now become necessary.

He gave her a little squeeze, stood up and kissed the top of her head, saying, 'I'll be back in a moment.'

Before returning, Philip collected two glasses and a bottle of sparkling elderflower drink. Back in his office, he placed them at a corner of his desk.

She made no sign of noting his reappearance. However, when he kissed her again, moved his chair fully against hers and boldly put his arm around her, still reading, she immediately snuggled up against him.

He turned his head and whispered into her ear. 'Can I pour you an elderflower drink?'

'That would be nice.' Still she did not look up.

Using his free arm, he poured some into a glass and put it close to her hand, where she clasped it. Still reading, she sipped from time to time.

Having got this far, there was a part of Philip that would have settled to sit there all night, meshed with her body and breathing in her essence, and yet at the same time he wanted more than this. However, he was aware of the risks inherent in trying to advance the situation. Up until now, she appeared to be in a kind of reverie, with him as a generic warm male presence, but he could not predict what might happen if he began to suggest more focused action.

He let the next twenty minutes float by, and then he made up his mind. He would push ahead – not without care of course – and see what headway he could make.

He nuzzled his face into her hair, murmuring. 'My dear…'

She was not distracted from her reading, but patted his thigh in a friendly way. 'Mr Thornton, I'm so grateful for the chance to study all this fascinating material,' she said affectionately.

'Please do call me Philip,' he invited.

'And you can call me Amanda.' She turned, gave him a large and beautiful smile, took his right hand in hers and shook it, announcing energetically, 'It's great to make a new friend.'

Philip was nonplussed. Although this turn of events was not unpleasant, it was not really what he had imagined would happen.

'Er… Yes...' He was almost stuttering. He swallowed, reconnected with his silky tones, and added, 'And maybe it's a friendship that could become deeper.'

'Of course it can!' she exclaimed cheerfully.

Philip jumped involuntarily at this sudden outburst, and Amanda looked at her watch.

'Goodness! It's got very late, and I've a long drive ahead of me tomorrow. Philip, I must go to bed now.' She sprang to her feet, gave him a quick kiss on the end of his nose, and was gone.

Philip leaned back in his chair in a daze. Then he pulled himself together and followed her at speed. But he was too late. As he reached the top of the stairs he heard the click of the key in the lock of Room 7.

Philip was in a paroxysm of torment. He had an urgent impulse to throw himself dramatically over the banisters in an attempt to relieve his feelings, but fortunately he realised that this was only likely to make things worse. Instead he ran back downstairs and into the kitchens, where he grabbed a selection of inexpensive crockery, put it in a box, and let himself out of a side door. Then he ran across the field behind the converted outbuildings until he reached the strip of woodland. He paused only briefly to catch his breath, and then, using all his strength, he threw each piece from the box at the trunk of a sturdy oak tree, smashing them and screaming as he did so.

It took about ten pieces before he began to feel a shift in his desperate state. Another five were smashed before he remembered that Amanda had been a regular visitor to *Field Fare*. Although he could not have her tonight, he had had more of her than before, and she was bound to return. He smashed the other pieces, picked up the box and returned to the hotel. After all, they were now friends. He somehow had to find the patience to build on that.

Despite this catharsis, once in his sitting room Philip could not resist rushing to the peephole, but the light was out, and there was nothing to see.

The following morning, refreshed, Amanda was the first to arrive at breakfast. Philip's sleep had been quite disrupted, and he felt below par, but he had had a cold shower, and was outwardly presentable. He had lurked under the stairs until he was certain she was coming, and then he had dashed to the kitchen to collect a pot of tea.

Amanda settled herself where she had sat for dinner the evening before, and gazed out of the window. A butterfly had attached itself to a bright flower that was not far from the outer sill, and she was fascinated by its movements.

Bearing the pot of tea, Philip walked briskly across to her, and greeted her warmly. 'Good morning, my dear.'

Startled away from her preoccupation, Amanda turned to see Philip smiling at her. 'Oh, hello!' she exclaimed. 'I had a wonderful rest last night. Thank you so much for everything.'

Although the dining room was empty, Philip turned his back to the room, kissed his hand, and then brushed it down her cheek. To his surprise and delight, she took hold of his hand and encouraged it to linger. The remaining tension inside him dispersed. So everything had been worth it after all – even the fraught scene in the woods. Other guests began to arrive for breakfast, and further intimate exchange was not possible, but what had passed between them that morning lingered on inside him, leaving him with a cosy feeling.

When it was time for her to leave, he helped her to put her things in her car, and then walked down the drive, where he waited beyond some shrubbery so that, unobserved by guests or staff, he could wave until she was out of sight.

Her next visit was surely only a few weeks away, and until then he had ongoing arrangements for the Ladies' Night to occupy his mind.

Chapter Eleven

The date of the Ladies' Night drew near. Philip felt confident about the success of the venture. After all, there had been so much interest in it that all the places had been booked up quickly, and there was a cancellation list of women who were so eager to participate that they had vowed to keep the evening free in case someone dropped out. All thoughts of Amanda had receded to the back of Philip's mind as he fantasised about which 'Lady' he might be drawn to on that night, and how he would arrange that she won the prize of a free night in Room 7.

He had decorations for the hall and dining room at the ready. There were masks based on those used in ballrooms of long ago, plumes of large coloured feathers, and some substantial framed prints of ballroom scenes. He had even managed to obtain a *chaise longue* to put in the hall. It was covered in upholstery of a deep red colour, and really did look the part – ready to receive a swooning lady. Maybe he should attempt to procure a small bottle of smelling salts?

Of course there would be no dancing during the evening, as men – except Philip himself – were not permitted to join them. However, he did plan a little discreet background music that suggested ballroom activity.

Philip's Ladies' Night would be based primarily on the consumption of a sumptuous meal – brought in by male waiters, who were there only to serve – followed by a number of well known party games. He was certain that everyone would have great fun. The Grand Draw would be made at the end of the evening. Guests would have purchased their tickets on arrival.

There were only two more days to go when Philip received an e-mail. It was from Amanda Adams. For a moment he wondered why the name seemed familiar, but as he read the message, he remembered with extreme clarity who she was, and he broke out in a sweat. She was writing to let him know when she was next passing through, and to his horror he saw that she wanted a room on the very day of his Ladies' Night.

Philip was greatly perplexed when faced with this impossible situation, and he paced round and round his desk as he contemplated his dilemma. While preparing for the Ladies' Night, any thoughts of Amanda had rapidly receded into the shadows as if she no longer existed, or perhaps never really had.

As his pacing grew more frenzied, Philip clutched his head in his hands. It seemed that he needed to do this to hold it together. But how could that be? There was no question about the stability of his skull. Yet his conscious mind felt as if it was operating in separate segments, and that somehow it would fragment completely. The situation was too much for him.

It was Philip's habit to keep the door to his office half open, but now he grabbed it, slid the sign on the outside to 'Engaged', and shut it quickly, locking it for good measure. Thus contained in the compact space of his office room he sighed, but the relief was only temporary. Pressure soon began to build up in his head again. He collapsed into his chair and leaned his elbows on the desk, while holding his head tightly in his hands. He had set his heart on finding someone new amongst the guests at the forthcoming event – someone with whom he could bring his fantasies into a shared reality, safe in the confines of Room 7, its cosy bed and its comfortable *en suite* bathroom. And now Amanda was going to descend and ruin it all. He had lost touch with the pleasures of being juxtaposed with her delightful body in this very room, and all he could think of now was how to get rid of her.

As these thoughts ran through his mind, the strange state inside his head slowly dispersed and he was able to think more clearly. This led him to believe that he was on the right track. Yes, he must find a way of ensuring that she did not arrive. Then a perfect plan came into his mind. He could reply to her e-

57

mail, saying that the main rooms were fully booked, and that unfortunately Room 7 was undergoing some essential refurbishment. That was it! Quickly he wrote the reply to her message and sent it off, having first included a link to another hotel more than five miles away.

After this Philip felt completely restored. He stood up, opened his office door, and went to resume preparations. Fleetingly, a memory of the pleasure of kissing Amanda's head flitted into his mind, but he pushed it aside and it vanished.

The Great Day arrived. Philip had spent the afternoon perfecting the decorations and conducting last minute checking with the kitchen staff. And now he was hovering in the hall awaiting the arrival of the first guests. He was wearing a new cravat that he had ordered specially for the occasion. Some weeks ago, he had spent more than an hour examining illustrations on upmarket websites, and had selected a stunning one. It was made of black satin and bore a pattern of a scattering of shooting stars. Right at the tip was an image of a small devil. This was a very clever addition, as no one could see what it was unless examining the cravat quite closely.

Philip had noticed on the same website that black satin sheets were for sale, and had been tempted to order some straight away. Instead he put the link into 'my favourites' and awaited delivery of the cravat, so that he could first check its quality. Since seeing it 'in the flesh', he had promised himself that not only would he order a pair of sheets but also he would order matching pillowcases. This would be something to look forward to after the conquest of that night.

Just then, a group of three party guests arrived. Each was wearing a long evening gown, so that progressing up the front step necessitated lifting the hem a little. This gave Philip a glimpse of three pairs of graceful ankles, and his mouth began to water. Word must have got out about the theme of the decorations, because one of the three was wearing a headband from which sprouted several large feathers, garishly coloured, and another was carrying an ostentatious fan.

Philip stepped forward to greet them.

'Good evening,' he said in his best purr. 'I'm the owner, Philip Thornton, but please call me Philip.' He held out his hand and gave each a lingering handshake.

'I'm Madeleine, and this is Coral and Olivia,' said one.

It was at this moment that Philip became aware that their gowns were made almost completely of satin. Madeleine's was a stunning orange colour, Coral's was a muted shade of turquoise, and Olivia's was a rich brown with a subtle pattern embedded in it. Although Philip's knees felt suddenly uncomfortably weak, his body felt strangely energised. He continued with his purring.

'Can I interest you in tickets for the prize draw?' he asked smoothly.

The three opened their purses and purchased a number of tickets, leaving their names on the backs of the duplicates.

'Of course, the money will go to a charitable cause,' Philip told them. At the moment he had no clue which that would be, but it didn't matter. Using names of familiar organisations, he could take a vote at the end of the evening.

He directed them towards the dining room, and they seemed to glide across the floor as one entity. Coral, the one with the fan, flipped it open, and using it as a shield, whispered to the others. Whatever she said provoked peels of laughter as they disappeared through the door. Philip was left contemplating how adorable it would be to have all of them in Room 7 that night.

A memory of Amanda's warm body came into his mind, unbidden. Philip bit one of his knuckles hard and concentrated his thoughts on the e-mail that had arrived yesterday. It had thanked him for the link, saying that she had booked in at that hotel, and that she would see him when she was next passing through. This was very reassuring, as it meant he could be completely certain that she would not show up unannounced. Aided by the sound of more guests coming up to the front door, he thrust the subject of AA out of his mind.

These five ladies were definitely much older than the first group, and by comparison their dress was drab and uninteresting. 'Almost frumpy' was the description that presented itself in Philip's mind. However, he decided soon afterwards that this was rather unkind, as the women themselves exuded a warmth and maturity that would enhance the general ambience of the evening. He welcomed them, and they bought a ticket each. Philip's purring was absent. Instead he presented himself as a kindly sort of person.

The next guest arrived alone.

'My companion couldn't come at the last minute,' she explained breathlessly, as if she had run at least a mile. 'I'm Belinda.' She giggled and added, 'Well, that's my name for tonight.'

She was wearing a diaphanous garment that looked rather fragile, as did her barely-camouflaged body underneath. The various shades of green of which her dress was composed complemented the colour of her hair perfectly, as it was a fiery shade of orange-red. Philip was sure that it must be have been dyed as he had never before encountered such a colour. It was on the tip of his tongue to ask if it was a wig, but fortunately two more guests approached and he was distracted.

He greeted the new guests, and sold tickets to them. The thin woman lingered until he had finished and then bought five. By the look of her skin she was young – perhaps not even twenty. She certainly wasn't a local resident, and he wondered where she had come from. He did not feel at all attracted to her. She was far too bony and her dress looked wrong.

One of the two new women – who were now in the dining room – had been wearing a cardigan covered in a pattern of birds, and the other had one with animals on it. Philip reflected that although not exactly suitable for an evening such as this, the design of those garments was surprisingly effective. Suddenly he shuddered involuntarily. It was as if a chilly wind had made its way through the hall. Then an image of his mother sitting knitting in front of the ancient inefficient gas fire in their tiny flat came into his mind so strongly that for a moment he thought she was there in front of him.

Determinedly he counted how many people had arrived. Eleven, and one that should have been there. That meant there were twenty-eight still to come. He went to the front door and looked out. Just then a minibus came down the drive and twelve women of varying shapes and sizes alighted.

He called across to them. 'Good evening, ladies. Please come this way.'

The task of ushering them into the hall and selling tickets took up all his concentration for a while, and for this Philip was grateful. By the time he had finished, all thoughts of that flat and knitting had dispersed. He hadn't had time to observe each of these guests in any detail, but his general impression was that they were all dressed appropriately for the evening, and that was sufficient.

After this, what appeared to be a convoy of three smart cars and a 4x4 vehicle arrived, bearing the rest of the guests. There was much bustle and chatter in the hall as he sold quantities of tickets. He was pleased to note that one of these guests had arrived with an elegant ball mask as part of her costume, another was carrying an old-fashioned cane, and another was wearing what was very obviously a rather dramatic wig.

When everyone was settled in the dining room, Philip made a short speech – thanking everyone for coming, and wishing them a pleasant evening. Soon the banqueting was under way.

It was while the *hors d'oeuvres* were being served that the last guest arrived. When Philip first noticed the latecomer, she was standing quietly just inside the door of the dining room. Although she was not attached to anyone already here, she appeared to be quite calm. She caught his eye, and he wove his way through the tables to greet her.

'Good evening. I'm Philip Thornton, your host for this evening.'

'I'm taking the place of a guest who had to drop out at the

last minute. I'm afraid I know no one here, not even the person who would have been her companion.'

Philip could hardly speak. Was she real? She was wearing a full-length black velvet cloak, and under it he could see a sheath dress of cream satin. Her shoulder-length auburn hair was held back with two combs, both of which were decorated with small precious stones that glimmered in the subtle light. The vibrance of her presence was almost too much for him. He blinked, almost expecting that when he opened his eyes she would have disappeared. But she was still there, unchanged. With enormous inner effort, he made himself speak.

'Would you mind sharing a table with the person who arrived alone?'

She smiled, revealing a set of white teeth, which were perfectly positioned. 'Of course not.'

'Can I take your cloak?'

She nodded, and he slipped it off her shoulders, his fingers trailing across the black velvet exterior and on to the lining. He knew instantly that this lining was made of satin of high quality, and it was all he could do to stop himself from burying his face in it. An image of the black satin sheets and matching pillowcases filled his mind, and he cursed the day when he had held back from ordering them.

The sound of her voice broke into his thoughts. 'I hired it for the evening.'

'An excellent choice,' he commented smoothly. Then he gestured discreetly towards the table where she would sit, and went to hang up her cloak.

All thoughts of the three women who had been the first to arrive had disappeared from Philip's head. The latecomer was definitely the one. Her clothes were right, her shape was right, and as no one here knew her, it improved his chance of success. It was most helpful that she had arrived last. He could be certain that she had not yet bought a ticket for the draw. He would attend to that very soon, and would ensure that hers was the winning number.

He grabbed the guest list, returned to the dining room, and made his way across to her. She was engaged in conversation with Belinda. He guessed that although the latecomer appeared to be quite mature, these two women could well be similar in age.

'Excuse me,' he began.

She turned her head and smiled.

'Can I take your details?' he enquired.

'My name is Crystal. Crystal Wakeling.'

'Could I have a contact phone number?'

'I'll give you my cousin's, because I'm staying at his house this week.'

Philip's hand froze for a moment, but as she dictated the number, he reassured himself that he wouldn't need to have a way of getting in touch with her. Everything would be achieved that night.

'Did you know that we're having a prize draw at the end of the evening?' he asked pleasantly.

'I think I did, but I'd forgotten until you mentioned it.'

'I'll bring you a ticket,' said Philip with alacrity. 'All proceeds will be in aid of charity.'

'What a wonderful idea.'

The sound of Crystal's voice was a new music to his ears. He went quickly to the book of tickets in the hallway, and tore out both marked 102. Then he scribbled her name on the back of one and thrust it into his pocket before taking the other to her.

'102. I like that number,' she mused. 'What are the prizes?'

'The First Prize is a free night in Room 7. But there are other prizes, too,' he added quickly.

Here Belinda broke in. 'Oh, I didn't know that. The leaflet I saw only mentioned the free night.'

'Since designing that leaflet, I decided to have a few other prizes,' said Philip truthfully, although he had only made that decision just over a minute ago. 'There will be a free dinner for two as the second prize, and some third prizes of a bottle of wine from my cellars. In addition, each guest will receive a small box of chocolates that have been handmade here at *Field Fare*.'

'That's very generous of you,' said Crystal, looking straight into his eyes.

Philip felt as if his inner structure was in danger of melting, and he knew that for now he had to distance himself. 'It's kind of you to say so. And now, ladies, please excuse me as I am needed elsewhere.'

The evening passed very pleasantly. The atmosphere among the guests was ideal, as there were frequent conversations between tables, as well as those at the tables where, in general, people knew one another well. Philip had arranged some simple entertainment between the main course and the sweet, and he introduced games while coffee was being served. The three satin women who had arrived at the beginning were now talking in a rather raucous way, which he found slightly disturbing, especially as their behaviour was likely to be a consequence of the fact that they had consumed extra wine. But any adverse impact on everyone else was entirely absent. In fact, the good humour within the gathering showed that they took it as if it were part of the general background entertainment. During the meal, Philip had slipped a number of treats to Belinda and Crystal, who responded as if it was all part of the fun.

At last it was time for the draw. Philip had folded up all the duplicate tickets and put them in a beautiful glass dish – a work of art that was usually positioned on the sill of his office. Ticket 102 was still safely in his pocket. He carried the glass dish to a side table, and banged on the tabletop to attract the attention of everyone.

Then he beamed round the room and announced, 'This is the moment you have all been waiting for.'

Everyone turned towards him, clapping and cheering.

'Third prizes first.' Philip picked out four of the folded tickets and read out the numbers. '53, 78, 10 and 92.'

The lucky winners showed their delight, and he informed them that the wine would be handed to them as they collected their coats.

'Second prize.' Philip made a great play of stirring the remaining jumble of tickets before selecting one. '55.'

The woman with the bird cardigan stood up. 'That's me!'

'Then we'll see you back here for your free dinner soon,' said Philip jovially.

Everyone clapped again. While this was happening, he carefully took ticket number 102 out of his pocket and held it crushed in the palm of his hand.

'And now...' Here he paused dramatically. He put his half-closed hand into the bowl and poked round several of the tickets with one finger. Then, in a way that he had rehearsed several times in the privacy of his office, he produced the ticket that he already held, as if he had just picked it up. 'The winner of the first prize – a free night in Room 7 – is the holder of ticket 102.'

Crystal gasped and her hand flew to her mouth. Then she stood up and announced, 'That's me.'

'Lucky you,' said Belinda enviously, although she was clearly pleased for her.

The rest of the people in the gathering smiled at Crystal, and some from the neighbouring tables leaned across to her and expressed their good wishes.

Philip spoke again. 'Thank you everyone for a wonderful evening. The vote on which charity to support will be counted when you have all left, but I'll post it on the notice board tomorrow. There's only one further thing. There will be a small box of handmade *Field Fare* chocolates for each of you to collect on the way out.'

The animal cardigan woman stood up and made a short speech of thanks to Philip and the staff of the hotel, and then everyone began to make their way out into the hall, collected their chocolates, and disappeared off into the night.

Belinda and Crystal were the last to leave. Philip fetched

Belinda's coat and Crystal's cloak, first taking time in private to bury his face into the gorgeous satin lining.

'That's great,' said Crystal as he helped her on with the cape. 'It's unblemished, so I won't have to pay any excess on the hire.'

'When do you think you might like to have your night here?' Philip asked carefully. He leaned towards her and added, 'I hope it will be soon.'

'I'll speak to my cousin and his family. I don't want to choose a night when they need a babysitter. I promised to give them babysitting in exchange for the week's accommodation.' She laughed. 'Their two children are as high as kites, desperate for the first evening when I'm in charge.'

This reassured Philip. He knew that he would not have long to wait.

Chapter Twelve

Philip was up early the following morning. Excited at the prospect of spending a night with Crystal, he had lain awake for a long time that night, but had woken feeling full of energy.

That morning, the hotel staff were exceptionally cheerful, and were chattering to one another about the success of the event. As soon as the receptionist came on duty, Philip gave her strict instructions that she was to let him know straight away when Crystal made contact to book her free night. This request did not seem at all out of place, as it was entirely appropriate that he should handle the booking himself.

Philip did not have long to wait. The eagerly awaited phone call came in the late afternoon. He was sitting in his office, gazing out of the window, lost in fantasies of a perfect night with Crystal, when the receptionist buzzed his phone. He picked it up.

'I've got your prize winner on the line.'

'Put her through.' There was a click, and Philip said, 'Hello. *Field Fare*, Philip Thornton speaking.'

'Hello Mr Thornton... I mean Philip. It's Crystal. I've phoned to book my prize night.'

'Hello, Crystal. It's good to hear from you,' said Philip smoothly. 'Now do tell me which night you want, and I'll make sure everything is ready for you.'

'I'd like to come on Thursday, if the room's free that night.'

'I can confirm that the room is certainly available, and I'll book it for you immediately.'

Crystal went on. 'There's one other thing. I won't be able to come until just after nine o'clock. I'll be looking after the children until my cousin comes home. After that he'll give me a lift up.'

'It's a great shame that you can't be here in time for dinner. However, I'll arrange some supper for you.'

'That's very kind, but I don't think I'll be able to eat much because I'll have had tea with the children.'

'I'll bear that in mind. We'll look forward to seeing you on Thursday.'

When Philip put the phone down, his thoughts were in a whirl. The situation was playing right into his hands. Under the circumstances it would seem quite natural for him to invite her to his sitting room for supper, and in that cosy environment he could assess her for further pleasures. Tomorrow was Wednesday. He could make his sitting room look particularly welcoming. It was already a pleasant place to be, but the addition of suitable flowers and decorative plants, strategically placed, would make it even better.

Philip spent that night lost in dreams of rapture. In the morning he took the unusual step of driving to the local town and selecting the necessary flowers and greenery himself. The shop packed everything securely, and once back at *Field Fare*, Philip rushed upstairs with each of the substantial cardboard boxes, eager to work on the adaptation of his room. One more item would arrive the following day – the bouquet he had ordered for Crystal, which he would place in Room 7. When everything was arranged to his liking, he went downstairs to his office, where he planned a tempting supper menu, composed entirely of bite-sized delicacies.

There was only one more thing to consider. Which cravat should he wear for the occasion? Late that evening, he looked through his entire collection, but found himself unable to make a decision. Ah! Now he had it. When she arrived, he would be wearing his best shirt, but it would be open at the neck. He could draw her into a playful task of identifying which one he should wear. This would be an ideal starter to their private supper.

On his way to bed that night, Philip took one of the small tables from the conservatory and installed it in his room.

It was Thursday evening. Philip had been hovering in the hall since ten to nine. He was rather glad that the last diner had left five minutes earlier, as this meant that he would not be distracted from his contemplation of Crystal's arrival. He was listening out for a car to draw up. At nine o'clock, he took a look out of the door, but there was nothing to be seen.

Philip was beginning to feel edgy. What if she didn't come after all? How would he cope? He checked his watch. Five past nine. Then he thought he heard a faint sound outside. He went to the door, and there she was.

'My cousin dropped me at the end of the drive and I ran the rest of the way.' She paused to catch her breath. 'I hope I'm not late.'

Philip stared at her. With her cheeks flushed and her hair blowing freely, she looked ravishing. Her slender figure conveyed with it a sense of vitality.

He had to work hard to suppress a tremble in his voice as he welcomed her in. 'Come in, my dear.'

She stepped into the hall.

'Can I take your coat?' he asked.

She slipped off her three-quarter length waterproof jacket, and he could see that under it she was wearing only everyday clothes, which somehow served only to enhance her beauty. She carried with her nothing but a shoulder bag.

'I hope you don't mind, but I've got a request for the start of the evening,' Philip began.

She smiled. 'That's fine. I haven't got any further than thinking about getting myself here on time.'

'As you'll see, I am without a cravat this evening, and I wondered if you would like to select one for me from my collection.'

Her face lit up again. 'That's a wonderful idea. I'd heard about your interest in them, and I'd love to see what you've got.' Her enthusiasm was obvious. 'Perhaps you could tell me the background to some of them.'

'Then would you care to share supper with me in my private

sitting room? The collection is stored there.'

'That sounds a wonderful idea. Thank you so much.'

Philip took her arm. As he led her upstairs to the door marked Private, he noted that her head was just above the height of his shoulders. They soon reached the door, and he guided her through it.

She gasped. 'The flowers are amazing!' She turned to Philip. 'Did you do this for me?'

Philip smiled down at her. 'It's a surprise part of the prize. You can take as many as you can carry back with you in the morning,' he added expansively.

'A few would be lovely,' she replied. 'My cousin has only a small house, and his children are quite boisterous.'

'Do sit down.' Philip gestured towards the couch. 'I'll fetch supper.' He moved towards the door, but then turned and added, 'I'll be back quite soon.'

When he returned, he was carrying a large open cardboard box. He set it down on the floor and lifted out several platters bearing a selection of cold foods, beautifully presented. There were also a number of small dishes.

He pointed to the first dish. 'This is a variety of game pâtés.' The arrangement of tiny pieces of pâté was surrounded by finely shredded mixed leaves. There was a plate of cheeses, and one of fruits. The other dishes contained sliced olives and various dips. Finally there was basket containing small bread rolls.

Crystal was clearly delighted. 'It's all so beautiful!' Then she added, 'I'm not sure how much I can eat, though.'

'Don't worry about that,' Philip said in a reassuring purr. 'Just take whatever you want. Now, you must tell me what you would like to drink. I can bring something up from the wine cellar.'

'I'd rather have sparkling water,' Crystal told him.

'Surely you'd like something a bit more interesting,' Philip pressed.

But Crystal shook her head, and he accepted her decision.

'I'll put the box of cravats on this chair, and then I'll go and fetch your water.'

He was soon back, and found her carefully laying out each of the cravats along the back of the couch.

'I've got to twenty, and there are quite a few still to go,' she commented.

Philip poured water into two large glasses and handed one to her. Then he tapped his glass on hers saying 'To the prizewinner. I hope you have a happy night here at *Field Fare*.'

Crystal's face glowed. Philip settled himself on the couch, quite close to her, and passed the dish of pâtés.

She took one and savoured it. 'This is truly amazing!' she exclaimed.

'One of our specialities,' said Philip modestly. 'Try one of the others,' he urged. 'I think I'll put this table next to you, and you can help yourself while I tell you some of the tales of the cravats.'

As time went by, Philip managed to make physical contact with her in a number of ways. He would sit closer to her, before getting up and walking about the room. Then he would lean over her, ostensibly to reach another cravat, apologising to her as he steadied himself by 'accidentally' putting his hand on her knee. He would also stand behind the couch and stroke her hair affectionately. She seemed to be absorbed in the storytelling, and although she did not shrink from his approaches, she did nothing to engage with them.

It was well after eleven o'clock when Crystal suddenly looked very tired, and her head began to nod.

'Would you like me to show you to your room?' asked Philip ingratiatingly.

Crystal chuckled. 'I think that would be the best thing, otherwise I'll fall asleep on this couch. I've had a wonderful time. Thank you so much.'

For a second, Philip was tempted to suggest that she lay down there and then, but he decided to continue to act his part, and took her along the corridor to Room 7. He unlocked the

71

outer door. He had left the inner door open, and the smell of the bouquet he had placed in the room had filled the space.

'More flowers!' she exclaimed, and she turned and gave him an unexpected hug.

Taken by surprise, Philip found himself holding her for rather too long, so that she had begun to ease him away before he released her.

To cover his confusion, he went across to the bathroom door and flung it open, saying unnecessarily, 'And this is the bathroom.'

Crystal put her bag down on the bed. 'This is a very pleasant room. I'm sure I'll enjoy my night here.' She took her mobile phone out of her bag. 'Can you tell me what time I have to be down for breakfast?'

'Any time between eight o'clock and nine thirty.' Philip was struggling to maintain his composure. He wanted only to grab her and force her on to the bed, but he knew that he must restrain himself. He managed to say, 'Er... I usually sit up late, so if there's anything else you need, don't hesitate to come and find me.'

'Thanks, but I usually go out like a light,' she told him.

What else could he do now but leave? He bade her goodnight, and retreated along the corridor. Then he dashed into his sitting room and almost flung himself against the wall by the peephole, trembling as he fitted his eye to it. But he couldn't see her! She had vanished. In his panic he nearly rushed out into the corridor to go and search for her, but then he realised that she was probably in the bathroom. Eye jammed tightly to the hole and shifting his weight impatiently from one foot to the other, he waited.

At last she emerged from the bathroom, wrapped only in a towel, the upper edge of which left her neck and shoulders completely exposed and barely covered her breasts. To Philip it was as if she were wearing a wedding dress. He wanted passionately to peel it from her and reveal everything beneath. He watched, transfixed, as she took a clean pair of pants from her bag, and slipped them on. After that she dropped the towel and picked up a baggy T-shirt from where she had laid it on the bed, putting it on over her head. Then she placed her mobile phone on the bedside table, climbed into bed and switched off the bedside light.

It was then that Philip made his decision. He lay down on the sofa, propping himself up with cushions, from time to time dropping the remaining morsels of game pâté into his mouth and imagining he was at a feast. Next he finished off the grapes. After that he stood up and went out into the corridor.

Outside Room 7, he paused to take several deep breaths before opening the outer door. His pulse raced, as by the low lighting from the corridor he could see that the inner door was ajar! Holding his breath, he put his head round it and looked across to the bed. He was about to take a step into the room when panic gripped him. Clutching his chest he backed swiftly into the corridor and retreated to his room, where he collapsed on the sofa.

It took some time before he regained his equanimity, but eventually he was able to think clearly again. He knew the exact nature of his objective, and without checking the peephole, he once more approached the door of Room 7.

He pulled the outer door nearly shut behind him, and this time he managed to step inside the room, where he could hear the reassuring sound of her gentle breathing. The very faint light that still penetrated into the room hardly reached as far as the bed, but in the gloom he could just make out where she was sleeping.

Little by little he advanced, making no sound at all, until he stood almost next to her. But at that precise moment, she took a deep breath, and began to turn in the bed. Like a terrified rabbit, Philip backed into the bathroom and thrust himself in the cupboard – the way into his secret room – where he almost passed out. His mind could cling on only to the necessity of becoming invisible, and it took some time before he could think beyond that. He did not have tools with which he could open the panel into the secret room, so he would have to face the awful prospect of somehow getting back across Room 7 and into the corridor beyond.

It took a long time before Philip could risk emerging from the cupboard. Even then he lingered in the bathroom, but hearing no sound at all, dropped to his hands and knees and began to crawl slowly across the floor of Room 7, towards its exit door.

He had nearly reached the door when he suddenly felt infused with energy and daring, and he stood up and began to unbutton his shirt. She did not stir. He slipped off his shirt and let it fall to the floor. Then once again he advanced towards the bed, although this time he made for the other side.

Silently, he contemplated his next move. He could lie down on the bed, or he could remove the rest of his clothes, and slip into the bed beside her. But there was a problem. If he were to take such action, the outer door must be shut and locked, and this meant that there would be no light at all.

Philip picked up his shirt and once again went back to his room, although this time it was with determined steps. He lay his shirt on the sofa, and searched in a drawer to find a tiny penlight that he knew must be there somewhere. His movements were purposeful, and soon he had it in his hand.

Once back inside the outer door of Room 7, he switched on his penlight before locking it. After that he entered the room and shut the inner door behind him. Although it was extremely unlikely that anyone would pass along the corridor at this time of night, he wanted to be certain that there was no noise transmission – either in or out.

Scarcely breathing, he first made his way to her side of the bed. What delicacy awaited him! She was lying on her back. Her aroma reached his nostrils and he almost fainted with desire. He put out one hand towards her face, and it caught the warmth of her breath. By the diffuse light he could see that her chest was rising and falling in delightful waves. The urge to pounce on her was intense, but sense prevailed and he restrained himself. Although he was convinced that interaction with her could bring only delight into her life, he did not want to startle her. She should become aware of him only slowly. Her face should show a sense of wonder, and then she should reach out to him and take him to her bosom. But for now she was fast asleep, and had no idea that he was there.

He watched her face closely. He could detect no flicker of movement that might suggest a change towards consciousness. He moved round to the other side of the bed, and was about to edge his way on to it when he changed his mind and instead began to loosen the fastenings of his trousers.

At this moment, she turned over and coughed. Philip dropped to his knees and hid his head below the level of the bed. There he remained, as if paralysed, oblivious of the acute discomfort that this was causing him.

Gradually the lack of any further movement from the bed encouraged him into a less cramped position. As he sat on the floor, rubbing his neck and his knees, he realised that he had no idea how long he had been in his frozen state.

Normal movement now restored, Philip contemplated the situation. He was so near to his quarry, and yet he was still a long way away from engaging with her.

At length, infused with sudden determination, he carefully slipped his half-naked body under the covers, taking care not to make contact with her prone form. And there he stayed.

As he lay there, his mind told him that he was being everything that he had ever wanted to be, while his body was on its back, motionless, his face in line with the ceiling. Those precious hours were filled with an ecstasy that he had never known before.

When the glow of his penlight trained on his watch revealed the time to be after half past five, Philip accepted that this night was at an end. But the bliss he now dwelled in was certainly not finished, and when he slid out of the bed, it was as if he were floating across the floor, out of the doors and into the corridor. Back in his sitting room, he occupied the exact position on the sofa as she had the evening before, and remained there until it was time to start work.

Crystal arrived at breakfast promptly at eight o'clock. Philip could see straight away that she was looking relaxed and refreshed, and he made his way across to her table, making sure that he did not hurry.

'Good morning,' he greeted her. 'I trust you slept well.'

'Like a log.'

He felt as if he was sinking into her smile, and had to grasp the back of a spare chair firmly in order to stay upright.

'I'm glad to hear that,' he said smoothly. 'At *Field Fare* we pride ourselves on ensuring our guests spend a peaceful night with us.'

'I'm sure I had a lovely dream, too,' Crystal confided.

Philip's grip on the chair tightened. 'What was it about?' he asked lightly.

She laughed. 'I can't remember, but I'm still enjoying some of the feeling I had in it.'

Philip said nothing else about it, and went on to discuss breakfast.

'I mustn't be long,' Crystal told him. 'I'll be walking out to the main road soon to catch the bus. I don't want to miss it, because there would be a very long wait before the next one is due.'

Philip stifled a desire to offer to drive her back to her cousin's later that morning, and instead brought her breakfast promptly.

Later, as he said goodbye to her outside the front door, she gave him another hug. It was just as impulsive as the first had been, but this time he managed to engage with it in exactly the most appropriate way.

Philip stood there until she was out of sight, and as he turned to go back into *Field Fare*, he had a sudden desire to leap up and click his heels together in sheer joy.

Success! He had shared a bed with a woman at last. Now his confidence would know no bounds. Remembering the wonders of the night, he would put Crystal out of his mind and plan his next conquest.

Chapter Thirteen

It was just over a week later when Amanda made contact again. She wanted a room for Tuesday night. This time Philip was ready for her. The confident glow in which he had dwelled after the other one had departed had not faded. He was glad that the receptionist was off that day, which meant that he made the booking himself. His e-mail confirmation said that she would be in Room 7, and that he was looking forward to spending some hours with her, reading through more of the old records. Another e-mail from her arrived later that day, which to his delight said that she, too, was looking forward to that. She added that she hoped to arrive early, so that if he were free they could make a start immediately after dinner.

Philip's already high spirits soared as he contemplated her arrival. It was now five o'clock on Monday, and in not much more than twenty-four hours, they would be together.

The next day he spent some time in his office, cleaning and tidying, and he brought one of the decorative plants down from his sitting room – one of those he had selected specially for the winner of the prize draw. Her name evaded him, but that was of little consequence. Soon Amanda and he would be together...

Philip was especially attentive to Amanda over dinner, although he took care not to neglect any of the other guests. When she had finished eating, he suggested that she took coffee in his office with him, an idea to which she agreed readily. He left the rest of the staff in charge of the dining room for the final half hour, retired to his office with a tray of coffee and mints, and shut the door, with the 'Engaged' sign in place.

With great ease, he confidently adopted the position that he had achieved with her when she was last there – his chair juxtaposed with hers, his arm around her, and from time to time kissing and nuzzling her cheek as they studied together. It was more a question of Amanda doing the studying and Philip doing something else, but she did not demur. She seemed to be entirely comfortable with their different occupations in this cosy tableau.

It was only his later suggestion that they share the bed in Room 7 that disturbed her composure.

She turned and looked him full in the face. 'Whatever for?' she demanded abruptly. 'We hardly know each other, and besides, you must be decades older than I am.' Then, without waiting for an answer, she resumed her studies.

Philip was taken aback. He had not expected this at all. He jumped to his feet, muttering about an urgent errand, and rushed off to gather his wits. As a much younger man, he had been very fond of smoking, but he had given up the habit before he was forty. However, now he was hit by a sudden craving for a cigarette. He grabbed a pack from behind the reception desk and hurried out into the night to find a private corner among the rhododendron bushes.

By the time he had finished smoking, he had decided on another ploy. Obviously something more subtle was required. He lodged a mint under his tongue to disguise the smell of the cigarette and returned to his office.

'I've found a really fascinating page here,' she greeted him.

So, there were no hard feelings. This was on his side. He sat next to her and pretended to study the section that she showed to him. It appeared to be about techniques of proliferating earthworms. He read a few sentences aloud to prove his interest. Then he closed the gap between their chairs and put his arm round her again.

Time passed.

'Do you have an early start in the morning?' he asked casually.

She replied almost mechanically. 'I'll be fine so long as I get away before eleven.'

'How about taking a nightcap with me upstairs in half an hour or so?'

To Philip's surprise, she accepted this invitation without demur.

'Would you like anything to go with it?' he asked casually.

'A chocolate or two would be nice,' she told him, not taking her eyes off the papers in front of her.

'Then I'll pop up and arrange it.'

Once out of the room, he darted upstairs and feverishly rearranged his sitting room, with the sofa positioned directly in front of the fire, which he turned on, ready. He lifted a number of bottles out of the cabinet and placed them on top, with the labels showing. Then he ran lightly back down the stairs to the kitchen, where he procured a selection of *Field Fare* handmade chocolates and arranged them on a silver dish.

Back in the office, he said, 'You'll probably have noticed that I have a special file for those papers. You can have access to them any time you're here.'

'Thank you so much!' Amanda exclaimed happily. 'That's so kind of you.' She paused for a moment. 'I suddenly feel quite tired. Can we have our nightcap, and then I'll get off to bed?'

Upstairs, Philip seated Amanda on the sofa in front of the fire, with the dish of chocolates near to hand. He was a little disappointed when she accepted only a small sherry as her nightcap. Realising that he had to keep his mind sharp, he poured a glass of ginger-flavoured water for himself. Then he sat down next to her.

To his great surprise, she kicked off her shoes, put her feet up on the sofa and snuggled up against him. Philip hardly dared to breathe. She seemed very relaxed, and took tiny sips of sherry, interspersed with nibbling at the chocolates.

'Oh! This one is rum-flavoured marzipan!' she exclaimed excitedly. 'My favourite.'

Philip thought for a moment as he weighed up the pros and cons of offering more. Then he said, 'There should be more downstairs. Shall I get you some?'

At this, she dived on him and gave him a kiss right on his mouth. 'My heart's desire,' she proclaimed.

Uncertain as to whether she was referring to him or the chocolates or both, Philip decided that the best thing would be to appear as if he was going in search of more chocolates and see what happened. He stood up.

'I'll give you a big hug and a kiss as a reward when you come back,' she announced.

Down in the kitchen, Philip counted the rum marzipan chocolates in the chilled storage. A hundred and fifty-four. Impulse drove him to feel that he should take all of them to her. Caution told him otherwise, but he felt quite unable to assess how many he should return with, and he sat down heavily on a chair to take stock of the situation. It took him a full five minutes to decide what to do. By then the solution had become obvious to him. He would take another four to her, and could return for more, later.

When he returned to his sitting room, he was startled to find that Amanda had disappeared. He transferred the chocolates carefully into the silver dish, and then discovered that she had been hiding behind the door, waiting to give him the promised reward. This turned to be delectable, and he found to his astonishment that he thrust his tongue as far into her mouth as he could. Meeting no resistance, he sucked a little of her saliva, and then stood back rather abruptly. Alarmed and rather confused by this turn of events, he concentrated on selecting a chocolate from the silver dish, and he fed it to her – slowly. This activity felt entirely comfortable and appropriate, and Philip quickly regained his composure.

They spent the night side-by-side, snuggled up on the sofa in its bed-shaped form. The experience of it was far beyond anything Philip had ever dreamed or imagined. He had no words with which to describe it. Amanda slept very soundly throughout, but Philip stayed awake, in wonderment, as long as he possibly could – absorbing the feel of the texture of the skin of her adjacent arm, while he breathed in her essence.

When morning came, Amanda roused him with a quick peck on the cheek before she jumped up.

'Where's the shower?' she demanded, and she laughed as Philip staggered to his feet.

'I'll let you into a secret, but first you've got to promise not to tell.'

She put a finger to her lips and nodded. Philip then proceeded to open the connecting door to Room 7.

'But that goes nowhere! There's just a piece of heavy material,' Amanda complained.

Silently, Philip drew it to one side.

Amanda gasped. 'That's Room 7!'

He patted her bottom. 'Off you go and use the shower.'

At ten fifty-five precisely, Amanda was in her car, ready to drive away, and Philip waited to wave her off.

'I told you I never share my bed with strangers,' she quipped. 'See you in a few weeks' time.'

When her car disappeared round the bend in the drive, Philip rubbed his hands together, and then went back into *Field Fare*. He had no doubt that by the next time she came his experience and expertise would have advanced considerably.

Chapter Fourteen

Feeling that all his inhibitions had evaporated, Philip's life went by in a most agreeable fashion. He soon lost count of the number of liaisons that he enjoyed. Some nights were for observations only – using the peephole. Other nights began with that, and then progressed to various scenes in Room 7, and yet others were spent with the opened-out sofa. He had resumed the use of the cordial, and hardly cared about the way in which he employed it. After all, he required any 'companion' to be safely unconscious in order that he could express himself to the full. Bodily contact during such times was unthinkable. It would merely serve to impede his freedom. He made no attempt to remember the names of his companions – all of whom were merely passing through.

Of course, Amanda was a little different. She reappeared every few weeks, and her name remained familiar to him, although it never carried with it any special significance. Although she knew about the connecting door between his sitting room and Room 7, he felt secure in the knowledge that her lips were sealed. However, in a corner of his mind, the realisation lurked that if she asked for a room here more often, he would have to find a way of ensuring that she transferred her patronage to a hotel some distance away. There was something about the idea of an ongoing relationship that repelled him, but in the circumstances he had created for himself he did not have to examine this.

And thus life could have continued on in this pleasing way for many a year, had not a chance meeting taken place…

Carrie had done very well on the hairdressing course, and the salon that had taken her on for a placement had subsequently engaged her services as a full-time permanent employee. Her ingenious creations drew a particular clientele, and her appointments were often booked up for weeks in advance. Carrie had a friendly, sociable personality, and the customers greatly valued the exchange of confidences that invariably took place. After all, hairdressing is such an intimate kind of service – one which engenders such trust.

One day, as she was working on a style for a relatively new customer, the woman made it plain that she wanted to share a dilemma.

'I'd like to tell you about something that happened to me recently,' she began, 'but I must ask you to keep it completely confidential.'

'I never breathe a word of anything anyone tells me here,' Carrie assured her.

The customer was probably in her early forties, and dressed well. As far as Carrie had gathered, she had been married for a number of years, and worked from her home as an accountant.

'My husband is often away – sometimes for several weeks – and although I have friends, I can feel quite lonely. I heard of an unusual hotel about thirty miles away. It has a very good reputation for ingenious menus for evening meals, frequently including game.'

Carrie said nothing, and continued creating the hairstyle.

The woman went on. 'Its name is *Field Fare*, and it's run by the owner – Philip Thornton.'

Carrie almost told the woman that she had worked there for a while, but instinct warned her not to divulge this information, at least for now. 'That sounds very nice,' she said in a neutral way.

The woman continued. 'I've dined there a few times, and I've found Mr Thornton very attentive.'

'Do you go with friends?' asked Carrie carefully.

'I went with two of my women friends the first time, but since then I've booked a single table. I never feel that I'm dining alone. Mr Thornton makes the evening so pleasant. He's even offered that I can use Room 7 any night I don't feel up to driving home after the meal. Isn't that kind?'

Without knowing exactly why, Carrie began to feel uncomfortable.

'Carrie, he's a most interesting man. He has such an extensive knowledge of recipes of bygone times. He even has his own secret recipe for a cordial. It's so exciting! His stocks are very low at the moment, but he promised I could sample some the next time I'm there.'

Her hand in the air, holding a comb, Carrie froze.

'Is something the matter?' the customer asked.

Carrie pulled herself together. 'No... not at all. I just thought I'd tangled a hair in the comb and didn't want to risk tugging it and hurting you. The hotel certainly sounds an interesting place.' She wondered what else to say, and then added, 'If it was me, I wouldn't be staying over. I prefer my own bed.'

The customer accepted this without comment, and the rest of the conversation was about local shops and the weather.

When Carrie returned home to her tiny flat that evening, she felt a bit under the weather. She decided that she would have a quiet evening watching a DVD, and then go to bed early. She didn't want to have to be off work, as she knew that her customers would be disappointed.

She loved this little place. It was only five minutes' walk from the salon, and it was situated over a flower shop, which meant that it was quiet in the evenings, and sometimes there was a subtle, exotic scent seeping up through the floor.

She had something light to eat, and then settled down to watch the DVD. It was a cheerful story of a family who liked to help all their neighbours, and she felt herself relax. She was in bed before ten o'clock, and read a chapter of her new library book before she settled down to sleep.

She had expected to wake feeling refreshed in the morning, but she spent much of the night tossing and turning, feeling worried and upset. The first thing she did when she got up was to take a long shower. It was as if there was a lot that had to be washed away, although she had no idea what that was.

Although she felt tired she didn't feel unwell, so she had some toast, made up her lunch, and set off to work. A ginger cat joined her on the way. It was very friendly, and kept weaving itself between her legs. She wondered where it lived. Surely its home couldn't be far away. She reached down to stroke it, and at that moment could hear a man's voice in her head saying something about a cat, and she shivered. Making no sense of what this was about, she quickly said goodbye to the cat, and continued on to her work.

Carrie didn't feel herself that day. When customers asked her if she was feeling all right, she said that she hadn't slept properly the night before, and that she was sure she would feel fine tomorrow.

When she got home that evening, things began to fall into place a little. That client who spoke about Mr Thornton had mentioned the cordial. Carrie had never forgotten that drink. Taking it in had been a strange experience, and one which she did not wish to repeat. If she were honest with herself, the next morning she felt as if she had been drugged. But why? Could Mr Thornton have drugged her? The idea seemed ridiculous. It made no sense. It was then that she remembered how the drugged feeling had been accompanied by an odd sense of something intangible that resulted in her taking a long shower as soon as she could.

Carrie slept well that night, and was back to her old self the following day. She thought of a couple of new styles to suggest to some of her clients, and for now she forgot about Mr Thornton and *Field Fare*.

It was when the client, Mrs Grainger, returned for her monthly appointment that the whole subject came back to her attention again. Carrie noticed from the beginning that this woman had an air of new excitement about her, and she soon found out why, as she could hardly wait to tell her what had happened.

'Carrie, that cordial is absolutely amazing stuff,' she began. 'Of course, Philip, er... Mr Thornton... won't divulge the recipe.' She took a deep breath and continued. 'I went for dinner again only last week, and sampled it. He had invited me up to his sitting room, because he keeps a bottle of it there. I can't put into words the exquisite taste, and the effect it has. I'm embarrassed to say that I must have had too much wine at dinner, because I fell asleep on his sofa, and when I woke the next morning, I discovered that he had kindly covered me up with a blanket and hadn't disturbed me. He's such a lovely man.'

'He's certainly a good businessman,' Carrie commented.

Her customer turned her head to look at her and asked, 'I'm sure that's true, but how do you know that?'

'I worked there for a while,' Carrie told her. 'I was saving up so that I could study hairdressing. In the end, Mr Thornton made a contribution by giving me overtime hours, and I left *Field Fare* a few months early.'

'That was good of him,' the client mused.

Carrie lowered her voice. 'I think I should be completely honest with you. He once gave me some cordial, and I passed out on his sofa – just as you did – and I think there was something wrong about it, but I can't remember what it was.'

Her client stiffened. 'Carrie, are you sure?' she asked in a tight voice.

'Cross my heart, I'm telling you the truth. I was glad to get away from the place after that, although I have to say he hardly noticed me after we'd made the agreement about my hours and the date I would leave.'

'I don't like the sound of this. I think it deserves some investigation,' the client said determinedly.

'Mrs Grainger, please don't mention my name,' begged Carrie. 'I've got good work here, and I don't want any trouble.'

'Don't you worry, Carrie. I'll think about this carefully, and I won't do anything straight away. I must say that on reflection his kindness towards me did seem to increase after I first mentioned that my husband is away quite often.' She paused, and then added, 'And please do call me Teresa.'

After this they both fell silent, and Carrie continued creating the hairstyle.

Then the client spoke again. 'If I'm to be scrupulously honest with myself, when I woke that morning, I had a strange feeling – as if I had been compromised in some way. Believing that Mr Thornton is a kindly and honest man, I had pushed it out of my mind, but now I've heard your story, I must think about it again.' She scrutinised herself in the mirror. 'Carrie, you're making a wonderful of job of my hair today. You can be sure that I'll be passing your name round my circle of friends. I think that your skills go far beyond your training.'

'I've always been interested in hairstyles, right from when I was really small.'

'You must have special intuition,' the client concluded.

The rest of the conversation was about quick nutritious lunch recipes. Then, her hairstyle complete, the client took one final look in the mirror, and smiled warmly at Carrie.

'I couldn't be more satisfied,' she pronounced. 'While I'm at the desk I'll certainly make another appointment for next month.' She opened her bag, took something from it and pressed it into Carrie's palm.

Carrie's face took on a look of astonishment as she saw it was a ten-pound note. She opened her mouth to protest, but the client shook her head and put a finger on her lips. 'You've more than earned it,' she stated firmly.

Chapter Fifteen

At home that evening, Teresa began to consider what she had learned from Carrie. She had had no time to think about it earlier, as she had been at a meeting with a new client all afternoon, and afterwards had found herself looking forward to advancing the work that it had produced for her. Grant would be away for another few days, and she had ample time now to focus on her thoughts about *Field Fare* and its owner.

She and Grant had been together for nearly five years. He was a wonderful partner, but they never had quite enough time together. What would he think about the whole situation? Teresa shook her head. Poor thing, he was so overburdened with work and the extensive travel it required that he wouldn't have any time for this kind of dilemma. She would have to deal with it herself.

Her thoughts ran on. Clearly Carrie was a very gifted young woman. 'I wouldn't be surprised if in a few years' time she's running her own business,' she said aloud as she patted her hair in front of the mirror in the hall. She smiled. 'Maybe later on I'll be her accountant.'

She went to the kitchen to prepare a light supper, which she ate as she watched the news.

'Now, back to that feeling I had after my impromptu overnight stay at *Field Fare*,' she murmured. She tried hard to recapture it, but whenever she thought she was close to it, it slipped away.

In the end she spent the rest of the evening working through a list of e-mails. Grant didn't phone, but he sent her a text to say that he was missing her, and she replied saying the same.

It was when she was getting ready for bed that the elusive feeling returned, hovering around in the periphery of her thoughts. Again she could not bring it into clear focus, and in the end she chose a book and concentrated on it until she was very nearly asleep.

She woke early the following morning. There were things she must do that day, but they would not fill up much of her time. Grateful for this, she stayed in bed, contemplating the possible mysteries of Philip Thornton and his secret cordial, and when she finally got out of bed, she spent a long time in the shower.

It was around ten o'clock when the phone rang, and she was delighted to hear the voice of Monica, one of her closest friends.

'Good to hear you. You've called just at the right time,' she said enthusiastically.

'I'm glad to have caught you,' Monica replied in heartfelt tones. 'I've something on my mind that I want to talk to you about.'

'Snap! We'd better fix up a chat soon.'

'Have you got any time today?'

'As a matter of fact, I have, but aren't you at work?'

'I'm off this week, so almost any time would suit me.'

'Do you want to come over here, or shall we meet somewhere for coffee?'

'You mean today?'

'Yes. Now, if you want.'

'I'll be with you in about half an hour.'

As Teresa waited for Monica to arrive, she wondered what her friend had to tell her that was so urgent. Monica was the kind of person who saved up her news until their next planned meeting, and Teresa could not remember a time when this had not been the case.

She did not have to wait long to find out. She heard Monica's car outside after only fifteen minutes, and she went to the door to let her in.

'I wanted you to be the first to know,' Monica burst out.

'Know what? Come in, sit down, and tell me all about it.'

'I've got a place,' Monica announced dramatically.

Teresa stared at her blankly. Her friend was talking in riddles, and drama was not her usual mode of expression. Then she began to realise what she might be talking about.

'You mean at uni?' she asked.

Monica nodded.

Teresa knew that for a long time it had been Monica's dream to study computer science at university, and that she had been saving as much money as she could, hoping that one day it would become possible.

'I didn't tell you I'd applied. If I hadn't got a place, I couldn't bear anyone knowing.'

Although she could understand what Monica was saying, Teresa was sad that she had felt that way, and said so. 'But I'm so happy for you! When Grant's back, we'll take you out for dinner to celebrate.'

Monica opened her mouth to protest, but shut it again when she noted the determined look on Teresa's face.

Teresa continued. 'And now let's drink to a long and happy future for you as a famous computer scientist.'

'But you know I don't drink,' Monica objected. 'And I don't know about "famous". "Competent" would do.'

'Okay, Competent Computer Scientist, and we can do the drinking with hot chocolate or herb tea.'

Teresa was so excited by Monica's news that she forgot about her own topic of discussion. She plied Monica with endless questions about the course until Monica put up her hand, saying 'Stop!'

Teresa was nonplussed. 'What do you mean? There's a lot to go through.'

'I know, but we can't do it all at once, and we've got to leave enough time for you to talk about your thing.'

'Goodness! I was feeling so excited for you that it had gone right out of my mind.'

'You'd better make a start,' Monica advised.

Teresa took a deep breath. 'It's a bit of a strange story,' she began. 'I don't know what you'll make of it. I'd certainly appreciate having your view on it.'

Monica sat quietly while Teresa told her the story of Philip Thornton, *Field Fare*, and what she had learned recently from Carrie. When she had finished, she waited for Monica's response.

'I've got something to say straight away,' Monica began, 'and I've got some questions.'

Teresa nodded. 'Go ahead.'

'You've got to tell Grant.'

'But I told you he's really overstretched at the moment.'

'You've got to tell him,' Monica repeated emphatically.

'Actually, I'm quite embarrassed about it all, and I'd rather he didn't know.'

Monica looked straight into her friend's eyes. 'You've *got* to tell him.'

'Okay. I know you're right.' Teresa picked up her mobile. 'I'll send him a text to say there's something we need to talk over, and that it's not urgent.'

'Perfect.'

Teresa sent the text off, and then said, 'What do you want to ask?'

'It sounds to me as if you and Carrie have had a similar, if not the same, experience. Has it occurred to you that there might be others, too?'

Teresa gaped at her. 'What an idiot I am! I hadn't considered that, yet when you say it, it's so obvious. Thank you so much for waking me up!'

Monica continued. 'If he's kept the ingredients of the cocktail a secret, it might be there's something in it that shouldn't be there. Have you thought about that?'

Teresa thought for a moment before replying. 'I would have been able to tell if it was very high in alcohol. There was some, but it definitely wasn't the main thing.'

'Maybe he's got hold of a concoction containing something like belladonna.'

'Mm… It's not impossible,' Teresa mused.

There was a pause.

Then Monica suddenly announced, 'I think there's got to be some research done.'

'Sounds good, but what have you got in mind?'

'Maybe we could put an ad in the local paper, asking for other victims to come forward.'

Teresa looked horrified.

'That was a joke,' Monica told her. 'But seriously, there must be something we could do. Perhaps I could do an experiment.'

'What exactly do you mean?'

'It would only have one new participant at first.'

'Who?'

'Me!'

Teresa's face broke into a slow smile. 'You mean... You mean you could go along to *Field Fare...*'

Monica nodded. 'I could book a table for dinner for one, and then go along and see what happens.'

'We'll have to plan it carefully. When will you aim for?'

'There's no time like the present. Besides, it would be good to fit in a visit while I'm still off work.'

Teresa stared at her. 'Are you *sure*?'

Monica took her diary out of her bag. 'Today's Wednesday... Why don't I phone to see if I can get a table for Friday?' She flipped through the pages. 'After that I'm quite tied up for a couple of weeks. Yes, I should definitely make an exploratory visit on Friday.'

'What if they're booked up?'

'Then I'll go along in the afternoon to acquaint myself with the place.'

Silently Teresa consulted the phone book of her mobile and gave her friend the number.

When Monica finished the call, her face had a satisfied look on it. She switched off her phone. 'You may have gathered what happened, but I'll spell it out for you. I got through to a receptionist, who said that they were fully booked for dinner on

Friday, but that she would ask the owner if a table for one could be squeezed in somewhere. She put me on hold, and when she spoke again she said that if I came for eight, they would definitely fit me in.'

Teresa could not help but grin. She was no longer feeling uncomfortable about this project. In fact, she was beginning to enjoy it.

'Grant won't be back until late on Saturday. Why don't you come here after your solitary dinner, and we can sit up talking about it. You can stay here for the night.'

'That sounds perfect.'

'You could call in here on your way to *Field Fare*, and we could put the finishing touches to your outfit.'

'Sounds fun.'

After Monica had left, Teresa received a text from Grant to ask if it was anything serious. Teresa couldn't help giggling as she replied to say that it could be highly entertaining... And she meant it.

Chapter Sixteen

Monica appeared in good time on Friday, and Teresa could not help but admire her outfit, which consisted of a simple figure-hugging full-length black dress with three-quarter sleeves, a short black velvet cape, and gold earrings with gold-coloured shoes and a small handbag to match. She wore her dark shoulder-length hair loosely.

'You look absolutely stunning!' she exclaimed. 'I'd like to do a bit to your hair, and then I must take photos.'

After adjusting Monica's hair, she fetched her digital camera and took pictures of the whole effect from several angles. 'I'll make prints while you're dining. It'll give me something useful to do while I'm waiting for the news.'

Monica looked at her watch. 'I think I'd like to get there early. I'll order a drink and pretend to read my book.'

'Be sure to have your mobile phone in your bag.'

'Don't you worry. It's essential equipment.'

'And don't hesitate to ring me. I'll be here every minute. By the way, what's your book?'

'I went to the charity bookshop in town to have a good look round. By sheer luck, I stumbled upon this small book of herbal concoctions.' She winked. 'If nothing else, it'll make a good stage prop.'

Teresa went with her to her car and waved her off. It was just into April, and although there was a nip in the air, there was a feeling of the days beginning to open out.

Having already studied the map, Monica found the road to *Field Fare* without difficulty. She turned into its drive, and although there were already quite a number of cars parked, there was ample space.

The entrance hall was warm and pleasantly lit. She gave her name to the receptionist, and was about to ask where the cloakroom was when a man whom she guessed was in his early sixties approached her. She noticed straight away that he was wearing a smart cravat.

'Good evening,' he said, holding out his hand. 'I'm Philip Thornton. Welcome to *Field Fare.*'

Monica found his handshake to be warm, and 'inviting' was the word that best described it.

'May I take your jacket?' he asked.

'Actually it's a cape. But yes, thank you.'

Monica watched him very carefully as he took it. For a moment it seemed as if her cape was much more important to him that she was. In fact he seemed to be scrutinising it, although she couldn't imagine why.

Inwardly Philip was feeling irritated. This cape did not have a satin lining. How annoying! He looked at Monica and smiled ingratiatingly. 'I hope that you enjoy dining with us tonight.' He handed a card to her, saying 'This entitles you to a complimentary drink while you're waiting for dinner to be served.'

'Thank you very much,' said Monica politely. Her eyes followed him as he crossed the hall towards the cloakroom, and again she felt that he was involved with her cape in some indefinable way.

She decided to order a small bottle of fruit juice. That way she could be certain that there were no 'additions' to her drink. She was delighted when she was presented with a familiar brand of organic apple juice and a beautiful glass, and she watched intently while it was poured out for her.

Philip had not lingered in the cloakroom. At first that woman had seemed rather attractive, but when he had encountered the lining of her cape, her allure had evaporated. However when he was on his way to the kitchen, instinct suddenly led him to turn on his heel, and he went to find her.

Locating her was not difficult. She was sitting in a snug

corner, reading a book and sipping from a glass. He glanced at his watch. Ten to eight. He could show her to the small table that he had squeezed in for her booking, or he could sit with her for a few minutes.

He went up to her. 'I hope the drink is to your satisfaction.'

Monica had not been reading her book. She had been watching out of the corners of her eyes, and had been well aware of his movements. She looked up, and feigned surprise. Then she said, 'Very much so, thank you.'

'Your book must be very absorbing,' Philip commented.

'It's fascinating. It's about herbal concoctions.' She looked at him intently and added, 'They can be quite beneficial, you know.'

Philip felt exposed. Was she really able to see inside his secret thoughts? Then he quickly pulled himself together. 'Er, over the years I have gathered together a large collection of old recipes.' He took a breath. 'We use some of them here,' he added carefully.

'How very interesting!' exclaimed Monica. 'Perhaps you could tell me about them.'

Philip hesitated only for a split second. All thoughts of the unsatisfactory cape lining had vanished. 'I'm rather tied up over the next couple of hours,' he began, 'but if you would like to join me for a drink after your meal, I would be glad to show you some of my collection.'

'Thank you, but I can't. I must be on my way soon after half past nine,' Monica replied. She scrutinised his face minutely, but could not see behind its mask.

'Perhaps you would care to sample the delights of *Field Fare* again on another occasion.'

'Maybe I will.' Monica's smile carried a teasing crinkle at the corners of her eyes. 'Perhaps the experience of your cuisine tonight will make it impossible for me not to return.'

Beneath his impregnable façade, Philip's teeth were clenched tightly. He had made up his mind that he would have her, but he had been thwarted. It was not enough that she *might* return. He wanted her, so she *must*.

'Let me show you to your table,' he said silkily.

He put his hand under her forearm as she rose, and guided her towards the conservatory.

As they entered, Monica gasped. 'How elegant,' she said in a low voice.

Philip's grandiosity was gratified by this, and he said expansively, 'I designed the layout myself.'

'Did you *r-e-a-lly*? I'm *so* impressed.'

Philip took her to a small table near to a large plant that partly concealed it, and screened it from the already subdued light. A single candle burned in a decorative holder. He pulled her seat back and repositioned it as she sat down.

Monica made a play of listening intently. 'Goodness! I imagine I can hear birdsong.'

'It's a very high quality recording that I play in the conservatory on certain evenings,' Philip explained.

'That is so clever of you. It certainly complements the ambience.'

Feeling that, after all, things were advancing satisfactorily, although not quite in the way he might have arranged, Philip now felt certain that she would return in the not-too-distant future.

'I must attend to the other guests now, but I will return to check whether or not the meal has been to your liking.'

Philip walked briskly out of the conservatory, and spent most of the evening in the main dining room, savouring the thought of introducing the new woman to his cordial when she came again.

Monica found that the food was truly wonderful. There was just sufficient glow from the candle, together with the light that found its way through the fronds of the neighbouring plant, for her to study some of the pages of her book between courses. By the time Philip returned, she was replete.

'That was a lovely evening,' she told him. 'I am certainly more than tempted to return.'

'You will be made welcome,' he assured her.

'I found some very interesting material in my book,' she confided, patting its cover.

Philip wanted to grab the book and check through it to see if there was anything about his cordial, but he restrained himself, and instead told her that he would fetch her cape. After retrieving it from the cloakroom, he found her waiting in the entrance hall. He spread it across her shoulders, went with her to the front door, and bade her goodnight.

Teresa couldn't help chuckling as Monica recounted the events of the evening.

'I think you've missed your vocation. You should have been an actress.'

'It's definitely computer science for me, but who knows, I might throw in some amateur dramatics.'

'Monica, you said there was something unusual about the way he handled your cape. Can you tell me more about that?'

'Not really. Why do you ask?

'It's just that it rings a faint bell with me somewhere. But it's so distant that I'm sure I wouldn't have thought about it had you not observed something.' Teresa fell silent for few minutes as she reflected. 'Oh… I think I might have it. I once saw him take someone's coat, and it looked as if he was examining the lining on his way to the cloakroom. In fact, now I recall it, he seemed to push his face into it for a moment. I remember at the time thinking that was a bit odd.'

'I must let you have a look at the lining of my cape,' said Monica. 'I think it isn't up to the standard of the rest of the garment, but it's never really bothered me because it doesn't affect its appearance.'

She handed it across and Teresa examined it. 'Mm… I see what you mean. It certainly isn't what you might expect. It ought to be made of good quality satin.' She grimaced. 'But if this is a clue to the goings-on at *Field Fare*, it's a pretty obscure one.'

'I've a gut feeling that it's significant, though. Maybe it'll become clearer in time.'

'Well, one thing's for sure. You've thrown out at least two hooks, and he's interested in both of them.'

Monica looked puzzled. 'There's the book, but what else are you thinking of?'

'Your outfit and your demeanour were obviously attractive to him.'

Monica laughed. 'I certainly tried my best.' She yawned. 'And now I'm worn out. Can we get off to bed? I've things I must see to in the morning.'

'Okay, but there's one last thing. When do you think you'll go back?'

'I'll have to let this settle before I decide.'

'You're very wise. I'm keen to push ahead with our research, but you're right. By the way, I had a text from Grant while you were out. He thinks he'll get back around lunchtime tomorrow.'

'That's good news. You'll have more time together.'

'And maybe we can talk about the events at *Field Fare* sooner than I had anticipated.'

Chapter Seventeen

The next day, Monica left before nine, and Teresa spent the morning buying food and tidying up. She was looking forward to seeing Grant, and was delighted when she saw his car turn into the drive just before noon. She jumped up and ran out of the front door to greet him.

'It's great you made it so soon,' she said as she threw her arms round him.

'I've been looking forward to this moment all week,' he told her, 'and I don't have to leave until Monday morning.'

Teresa's face shone. 'How did you manage to fix that?'

'Something was postponed, and I did a bit of juggling as well. Let's get my things in, and I'll get changed. I'd like to get out for some fresh air. Being cramped in a car isn't ideal.'

'Okay. Do you need anything to eat?'

'No, not yet. Let's go for a walk.'

Ten minutes later, they were heading for the path along the river.

'What a relief,' said Grant as he breathed the clean air.

They walked along together in silence for a while. The sun was shining, but there was still a nip in the air.

After a while, Grant asked, 'Do you mind if we do the full circuit?'

Teresa knew that he meant a walk of more than six miles, and that they would return to the house by a different route.

'I was hoping you'd suggest that,' she replied, 'but what are we going to do about lunch?'

'Can you wait until we get back to the house?'

'No problem.'

As they progressed, the inner tension Teresa always carried when they were apart dispersed. She felt at one with Grant and with the world.

'I've some news about how work is likely to evolve over the next six months,' Grant told her. He went on to explain the details as they covered the next mile or so.

It was after lunch, when they were relaxing in the sitting room, that Grant turned to Teresa and said, 'I'd like to hear about what prompted that text you sent yesterday.'

'Are you sure? There's no rush.'

'I'm curious.'

'Before I begin, I want to you know that I feel I've been a complete idiot.'

Grant raised one eyebrow quizzically, and waited for her to begin.

As Teresa told him the story, he said nothing until she had recounted most of the second of her conversations with Carrie, the hairdresser.

Then he sat bolt upright, and said angrily, 'It's obvious he's a complete bastard! What the heck does he think he's playing at?'

Teresa was honest. 'I'm certainly partly to blame for what happened to me. I shouldn't have put myself in that situation. Grant, I can miss you so much that sometimes I try to make myself not feel it, and that's how I made this mistake.'

Grant reassured her. 'It was perfectly okay to eat out at an unusual venue. Why on earth shouldn't you? I'm only sorry you didn't see the writing on the wall when he invited you to a private tasting of his cordial. The whole thing stinks.'

'Yes, I agree. I was drawn in because I had been feeling lonely, and that made me too interested to learn more about the special drink.' She paused for a moment before continuing. 'Grant, there's something else I should say about what passed between Carrie and myself.'

'On you go.'

'Each of us had a vague sense that something wrong had taken place when we were not conscious.'

Grant punched the arm of the chair in fury. 'Just wait until I get my hands on the rat!' he raged. 'He's a criminal!'

'If you're thinking of the worst, I can say I'm absolutely sure it didn't happen,' said Teresa flatly.

'How can you be certain?' Grant was sitting on the edge of a chair, his body tense, like a coiled spring.

'No mess.'

'No mess?'

'None.'

'Nowhere?'

'No mess anywhere.'

Grant looked less tense, but was clearly still very worried. 'What do you think happened, then?'

'I've tried and tried to remember. I've a sense of something odd going on around me. That's all I can say.'

'Where does Carrie work? I want to go and talk to her.'

Teresa was horrified. 'You can't do that! I promised her that everything she told me was completely confidential, and she's very worried about anything getting in the way of her career.'

Grant looked straight into Teresa's eyes. 'Don't you realise that the countryside is probably littered with people who have been through something similar at the hands of Philip Thornton?'

'That's what Monica said, and I could see immediately that she was right. Grant, there's more of the story still to tell, and before I start, I should let you know that you don't need to grip the arms of the chair like that.'

Grant looked at his hands. All the knuckles were white. Slowly he relaxed his grasp and leaned back.

Teresa continued. As she told Grant everything about the plan that she and Monica had made, and how far the research had progressed, she saw his face lose its tense state and a broad smile replace it.

When she had finished, he winked at her.

'What exactly does that signify?' she enquired.

'It means that I'm impressed by what you two have been up to, and that I want to join in.'

'How?'

'I think that you and I should go and have a cosy dinner for two at *Field Fare* quite soon.'

'When are we going to be able to fit it in?'

Grant looked at his watch. 'I expect if I phone for this evening, I'll find they're fully booked, and I don't think Philip Thornton would bother to squeeze an extra table in for a couple. In any case, I'd like an evening at home. However… I could ring and see if we can eat there tomorrow. What do you think?'

Teresa nodded vigorously. 'Go on.'

Grant picked up the phone, and made the booking. Then he said in a serious voice, 'Of course, you do understand that because I have to leave promptly on Monday morning, we won't be able to stay on to sample Mr Thornton's cordial.'

Teresa kicked his leg affectionately.

When they were getting ready for bed, Grant suddenly clapped his hand to his mouth in mock alarm. 'What shall we wear tomorrow evening? I don't have a dinner jacket.'

'You'd better wear a tie,' Teresa mused. 'Oh, wait a minute… Philip seems to have a penchant for cravats...'

'I'll see if I can dig mine out.' Grant dived at his chest of drawers, and burrowed around. Then he stood up, triumphantly waving the ancient cravat he had been given by a friend many years before. 'I knew this would come in handy one day,' he announced.

'No you didn't,' Teresa challenged, giving him a playful push.

Grant pretended that she had thrown him on to the bed. 'You can take me,' he told her seriously. 'I won't resist.'

At this they both spluttered with laughter and then lay close together all night.

Chapter Eighteen

Grant and Teresa were arguing good-naturedly.

'I think you should wear some ostentatious jewellery,' said Grant.

'I'd feel silly.'

'That's not the point. We're trying to flush out what's going on, and the best way of doing that is to ring the changes.'

'But all I've got is some really heavy stuff from Granny's sister, and you know I never wear it.'

'Let me have a look.'

'Okay.' Teresa took an ornate box out of the bottom drawer of her chest, and placed it on the bed. 'You can choose.'

Grant began to sort through its contents. 'This one looks good,' he said as he pulled out a heavy pendant. 'It'll go well with your satin gear.'

Teresa spluttered. 'Okay...'

'Oh... and...'

'And what?'

'You could pretend I'm your boyfriend.'

Startled, Teresa stared at him and then exclaimed, 'What fun!'

Grant grinned mischievously. 'And it might well throw him into a state of confusion.'

They arrived at *Field Fare* at seven o'clock. Grant made a show of helping Teresa out of the car in a gentlemanly fashion, and they went into the entrance hall with her arm linked through his. They approached the reception desk.

'I booked a table for two. The name's Grainger. Grant Grainger.'

'Ah, yes, sir. I took the call myself. Would you like to go

into the lounge, and I'll get someone to take your orders for a drink?'

Just then, Philip appeared. 'Good evening,' he began, 'can I take your...' He recognised Teresa, froze momentarily, and then gathered himself, '... coats.'

Teresa had deliberately left her jacket unbuttoned. Grant watched as Philip's eyes became glued to her pendant, which was barely visible above the 'V' of her plunge neckline. Slowly Teresa removed her jacket.

Saliva was building up in Philip's mouth, and he tried to swallow, but found he couldn't. The deep ruby red of the lining of the jacket matched the colour of her dress exactly, and he was certain that the lining was made from *satin*.

'I haven't brought a jacket, but I'd be obliged if you could take my partner's,' said Grant studiedly, making a deliberate show of adjusting his cravat.

It was then that Philip noticed it, and it riveted his gaze. It was the most amazing design that he had ever seen, and he wanted to grab it instantly, and make off with it.

He tried again to swallow, but failed. He could not speak, as the quantity of saliva that had gathered in his mouth had reached a critical level. He grimaced in as warm a way as he could muster and took the jacket, but when his fingers touched the satin lining, he was well nigh lost. He turned and tottered towards the cloakroom in a state of disorientation.

Teresa put her mouth to Grant's ear. 'I think we've made an impression on him already,' she whispered.

'Darling, let's choose something special to drink tonight,' said Grant, loudly enough to be easily overheard. He guided her attentively through the door to the lounge, and they sat close together on one side of the welcoming log fire.

Having emptied his mouth into his handkerchief and enveloped his face temporarily in the ruby red satin, Philip felt able to leave the cloakroom. He returned to the hall just in time to see Grant and Teresa moving as one, as they passed out of sight.

His head felt as if it were spinning. What was happening? Why had she come here with *him?* Desperate, he told the receptionist that he had to go upstairs for half an hour, and that he mustn't be disturbed.

He ran up the stairs, dashed through the Private door, locked it, and then flung himself on his sofa. He had been disturbed more than he had been able to admit to himself when that new woman had come on Friday. She had been stunningly attractive, and she had a book about herbal concoctions. However, she had worn a cape that had no satin. It just didn't add up. And to cap it all, she didn't stay on to drink his cordial. And now, one of his earlier companions had arrived, looking radiant, with man younger than he. She was wearing a jacket lined with the *best satin that he had ever encountered*, and the man was *wearing a cravat that he wanted for himself.*

Everything had been going smoothly – perfectly reliably, according to his impulses and plans – but now all seemed to be going awry. This had caught him completely off guard, and he felt dreadful. His whole body was trembling with shock. He wished that he had not sealed off his secret room. He had become so sure of his pleasures around females that he had left his womb room behind. If only he could be in there now, slipping amongst satin sheets and creating a world in his mind that was entirely consistent, then perhaps he would feel restored.

What could he do? Maybe the cordial would help… Yes, that was it. He stood up, found the bottle, and with shaking hand, poured a small quantity into a glass. Just one sip… It's very potent… Only a sip…

Downstairs, Grant and Teresa were choosing a starter and a main course. They were making a play of appearing as new lovers, and they were doing it extremely well.

Another sip… Several deep breaths… One more sip. Philip's body began to feel less unstable. He tore off his cravat, went to his collection, selected the most expensive one and put it on, checking in the mirror to ensure exact positioning. He washed his hands, scrubbed his already clean fingernails, patted himself dry on his favourite satin-edged towel, and went out into the corridor, now feeling able to face the dining room. He was profoundly glad that this Sunday was relatively quiet. Not all of the tables were in use, and he had not opened the conservatory.

Outside the dining room door he paused and took a very deep breath before entering. The first thing he noticed was that *she* was nuzzling her boyfriend's neck. He stopped dead in his tracks. It hardly mattered that she was doing it discretely, and no doubt none of the other guests had noticed her actions. The important thing was that *he* could see, and that this undermined his newly regained poise. He stepped backwards out of the room. Once in the hall, he made for the kitchen with speed.

Trying his best to conceal his frenzy, he made straight for the fridge where milk, yoghurt and cream were stored, snatched a carton of double cream, stuffed it into his pocket and hurried to the stairs, which he ascended two at a time. In the safety of Room 7, he pierced a hole in the lid of the carton, pressed it to his lips and lay back on the pillows of the bed.

Downstairs, Teresa whispered to Grant. 'I think we're putting on a good show, but I've hardly seen anything of Philip.'

Grant chuckled. 'I bet it's *because* we're putting on a good show that we aren't seeing much of him. I last caught sight of him when you were nibbling my ear lobe. He backed out promptly. You should have seen his face.'

Teresa giggled.

Grant put a finger on her lips. 'Sh... You don't want to spoil it.'

Teresa glanced towards the doorway, just in time to witness Philip's return. He was carrying a small tray, but she couldn't see what was on it. He made no overt sign of being affected by her. He went to the nearest table and left something there, and then he disappeared again. She watched covertly as he came back again, approached another table, left something, and went away, repeating this sequence until he had visited every table but theirs. She wondered what would happen next.

When he returned with the tray, he lingered in the doorway

for a few seconds and then made his way towards them. She detected a change in his gait. It was as if his legs had become quite heavy. As he approached, she turned her head towards him.

'I trust that dinner has been to your satisfaction,' he said, almost mechanically.

Grant turned his seat so that he was almost facing Philip. 'You must compliment the chef for us. It was a stunning experience.'

Philip felt a little less threatened, and managed to say 'I hope that you might return some time. The menu is changed every week.'

'I work away from home quite frequently,' said Grant, emphasising each word slightly, 'but we may well return. An experience like this is not found easily elsewhere.' He pressed his foot down hard on Teresa's.

Teresa thought that she was going to explode with laughter, but bit her tongue hard to distract herself.

Philip went on. 'I see you are wearing a most elegant cravat. Cravats are one of my special interests.'

'A friend obtained this one for me. I believe the design has an unusual history.'

Philip did not ask for details of this, and instead he told Grant the story behind the design of the one that he himself was wearing. After that he felt a little better, and took a small dish of chocolates from his tray and put them on the table.

'Oh good!' exclaimed Teresa. 'I can see one of my favourites.' She stopped, and then said to Grant, 'They're made on the premises.'

Philip looked as if he had been struck. Grant feigned a mixture of astonishment and dawning outrage.

'Please feel free to take your time enjoying them,' said Philip, backing away hurriedly. 'I have things to see to.' Then he fled.

Grant made a play of dusting his hands off. 'I think that's probably sufficient for this evening. I can wrap the chocolates in my handkerchief if you don't want to eat them all now.'

'One chocolate, and then we'll leave,' Teresa decided.

They went to collect her jacket from the cloakroom, and Grant was about to help her on with it when he noticed a mark on the lining.

'What's this?' he asked. 'It wasn't there when we left the house.'

'How odd,' Teresa replied, 'and it's damp.'

On the way home, Teresa savoured the events of the evening. 'I can't wait to tell Monica about it all. You were wonderful!'

Grant patted her thigh. 'You didn't do too badly yourself.'

Chapter Nineteen

The next time Grant was at home, he and Teresa had spent their time sourcing materials for redecorating the spare bedroom. They both enjoyed taking care of their house, so such tasks were always a pleasure.

More than two weeks passed before Teresa and Monica could get together again. Teresa had updated her friend on the phone, and Monica had laughed until tears rolled down her face. Apart from that, Teresa had been very busy with her work, as she had acquired several new clients whose tax year finished in April and who wanted some early feedback about figures.

Now it was time to lay their plans for Monica's next visit to *Field Fare*, and they had arranged that Teresa would go round to Monica's flat on Wednesday evening.

'I've something to show you,' Monica told Teresa as she let her in. 'I've been doing a bit of searching around on eBay, and I've come up with something that might suit our theatrical pursuits. I was thinking of placing a bid, but first I want to see what you think of it.'

'You've been busy,' Teresa remarked.

'Amongst other things, the subject has been on my mind quite a lot.' Monica took Teresa to her laptop, which she had open on the dining table. 'I'll bring it up.' It was not long before she turned the screen so that Teresa could see it. 'That's as big as I can get it.'

'Mm... It looks really good, but of course we can't tell properly until we can feel it and try it on.' Teresa read out the description. 'Shawl... hand-embroidered... lined with satin...' She turned to her friend. 'It must be pretty unusual to have a shawl that's lined with satin.'

Monica nodded. 'I've certainly never come across one

before.'

'Why don't we just go for it? I'll share the cost with you. Let's agree a bid and see what happens.'

The bid placed, they went on to discuss Monica's next outing to *Field Fare.*

'He'll be keeping an eye open for your booking, and he'll expect you to stay on to drink cordial with him,' said Teresa.

'I've put a lot of thought into how to handle it,' Monica mused, 'but I expect I'll have to make much of it up as I go along.' She paused, and then said, 'I've been wondering what I'll do if he pounces on me.'

'How about slapping him round the ears saying, "Get thee hence!" or perhaps "Unhand me, you foul brute!" '

'Perfect!' exclaimed Monica, holding her sides as she shook with laughter. 'The only problem is that I might spoil it by giggling.'

'Seriously, though, you'd be quite within your rights to whip out your mobile and phone the police. But to be honest I don't think he'll make such a move.'

'Why are you so sure?'

'He doesn't seem the type. He's more the sort of person who spends time thinking how wonderful he is, but wants a woman in the room while he's doing it.'

'You mean he's a genuine descendant of Narcissus himself, and the only thing that's different is that he isn't gazing into a pool while he's admiring himself?'

'You've got it.'

'And no one ever sees him while he's in the full-blown version of the self-admiration…'

'I imagine not.'

'You mean he wants a presence, not an audience. But if I wanted to witness it, I could pretend to drink a whole glassful of cordial, pretend to pass out, and then wait…'

'An interesting idea.'

'Frankly, though, I'm not sure I want to,' Monica reflected soberly. 'And what if he takes me by surprise by not giving me any cordial and suddenly changing the goalposts?'

'Mm… the more we think through this, the more my view is that you need an accomplice who's stationed nearby. That way, if you get into a sticky situation, you can say you need the bathroom, lock yourself in, and then phone for immediate assistance.'

Monica sighed with relief. 'That's more like it. The whole venture is beginning to sound a bit more feasible.' She paused before continuing. 'But who's going to be the accomplice?'

'Me, of course.'

'You?'

'Yes, me.'

Monica considered this. 'Maybe it should be someone who's got experience as a bouncer.'

Teresa giggled. 'There's nothing I'd like better than to see Philip Thornton being thrown out of his own front door, but to be honest I don't think it'll be necessary. I can lurk in my car outside, and if you send me an SOS, I'll be there in a trice. The mere sight of me advancing up the stairs of *Field Fare*, relaying the scene to Grant on my mobile, will be enough to paralyse him.'

'Mm… I think we should run this plan past Grant.'

'You're probably right. It's just that the idea of a pair of women defeating Philip Thornton is very appealing.'

'I agree, but building in a safety net should be part of any sensible strategy. In any case, Grant might want to be part of it. When you come to save me, he could be sitting in the car, at the ready, in case we need backup.'

'In that case we won't book your next dinner date until I've had a chance to discuss everything with him.'

Having decided this, the conversation went on to other interests, and it was after midnight by the time Teresa left for home.

Two days later, Teresa received a text from Monica to say that their bid had been successful, and the shawl should be delivered the following week. Grant arrived home the next day, and he and Teresa had a long talk about Monica's proposed dinner date. He was adamant that she and Monica should not be dealing with this alone, and it was agreed that the next visit should be made at a weekend when he was available. Having consulted his diary and identified a couple of dates, they sent an e-mail to Monica. Before the weekend was past, a date had been set.

On Thursday of the next week, Teresa found a phone message from Monica. She sounded jubilant.

'It's arrived! Our shared shawl is truly amazing. I can't wait for you to see it, and I'm going to find it difficult to sit out the next nine days until I can put it into action.'

The planned day arrived at last. It had been arranged that Monica would come and join Grant and Teresa for lunch, and that they would spend the afternoon perfecting her appearance.

She arrived promptly at noon, with a flight bag on wheels. Grant greeted her at the door.

'Good to see you. Come on in. Let me give you a hand with that.'

'It's all right, thanks. It's not heavy.'

Monica brought the bag into the sitting room, and Teresa was eager to see the shawl straight away.

'Don't worry,' Monica assured her, 'I'll get it.' She opened her bag, took out the shawl, and held it up.

'It's completely stunning!' Teresa exclaimed. 'The purple velvet is an amazing shade, and the embroidery is out of this world. And all this complicated gold braiding on the edge is...'

'Stupendous,' Grant finished for her.

'Feel the quality of the materials,' Monica told them. 'The visual impact is incredible, but when you add the sensory one, you've got a feast.'

Teresa took it and wrapped it round her shoulders.

'Anyone wearing that wouldn't need to wear anything else,' Grant remarked with a completely straight face.

Teresa slapped him affectionately. 'You and your clever

ideas…   Well, certainly the satin lining is particularly voluptuous, and would feel good on bare skin, but it doesn't come down far enough. Monica, what have you got to go with this?'

'I've brought a couple of things. I'd like your view on which would suit best.' She pulled some items out of the bag. 'There's this crocheted dress, and here's a skirt and blouse.'

Teresa admired them. 'You've got some really nice things here.'

'Yes,' agreed Grant, 'either kit would be fine.'

Teresa had a different reaction. 'On balance, I'd go for the skirt and blouse. The skirt matches the shawl almost exactly, and the lilac shade of the satin blouse brings out a similar colour in the decorative needlework on the shawl. But why not put them on to give us the full effect?'

'Okay,' replied Monica cheerfully. 'I'll do a fashion show.'

When she appeared wearing the skirt and blouse, Grant blew a wolf whistle. 'Why can't we ditch the *Field Fare* engagement and the three of us go out somewhere nice?'

Teresa stood on his big toe as heavily as she could.

'Yeow!' he shouted.

Teresa scowled at him. 'That's what you get for going back on your word.'

'I was only teasing.'

'I think I should let you see me in the crocheted dress before we make the final decision,' Monica advised.

She was back in a few minutes.

'You look great in it, but it isn't quite as good as the other gear,' Grant decided.

'Right,' said Teresa briskly, 'now that's sorted out, we'll have lunch and then I'll get to work on your hair.'

The afternoon passed pleasantly as they all contributed to Monica's appearance. The final touch was a pretty clasp that Teresa added to her hair.

'Perfect!' Grant approved. 'Photo shoot next.'

Seven thirty saw Grant drawing up in a far corner of the car park of *Field Fare*.

'This overgrown rhododendron bush is quite handy,' he observed. 'Off you go now, Monica.' He let her out of the back of the car and gave her a quick kiss. 'You'd make a great secret agent,' he whispered as she left.

Then he and Teresa switched on their mobile phones and waited.

'It's going to be ages before she's likely to ring,' Teresa commented.

'I know, but we can't be certain of anything.'

'Perhaps we could stroll up the drive?'

'I'd thought about that, but we mustn't do anything to attract attention to ourselves.'

'Maybe we could take it in turns to push our way amongst these bushes.'

Grant considered this. 'Possibly, but only with mobile in hand.'

'Of course. I wouldn't consider it otherwise. We've got to be able to keep in touch at all times.'

This expedient passed nearly an hour away, but eventually they tired of it.

Then Grant had an idea. 'We can cover ourselves up on the back seat with the pile of blankets I brought and play "I Spy".'

Inside *Field Fare* things had been going entirely according to plan. Philip had been waiting for this moment all afternoon. He had stationed himself at reception by leaning casually on the desk and conducting inconsequential conversation with the receptionist. When he saw Monica enter the hall, he glided across to her.

'May I take your coat?'

'Thank you, but no. This shawl is part of my outfit.'

Philip was caught between two sets of feelings. He could now see the lining of that shawl, and he wanted to be alone with it. Yet if he left her with it – as she desired – it meant that she would bring it with her to his room, later. Then his heartbeat became quite unsteady when he observed that not only was the lining of her shawl made of satin material, but also her blouse!

He swayed momentarily, gathered himself, and said, 'Let me get you a drink.'

'I'd like a glass of lemonade.'

'We make it on the premises,' he replied in his best purr. 'Take a seat in the lounge, and I'll be back in a moment.'

When he returned, he was carrying a tall glass of almost clear liquid.

Monica took a small sip from the glass. It tasted fine, and she decided that it was quite safe to drink it.

'Thank you. It's very refreshing.'

'We're rather busy tonight,' said Philip, 'but I'll come past your dinner table at times to check that you're happy with the meal.' He stopped and cleared his throat before adding, 'Would you like to take up my invitation for a glass of cordial in my rooms later on?'

Monica inclined her head invitingly. 'Of course,' she replied in a low voice. 'And I have my book with me again this evening.'

'Ah, I'm glad to hear that. I had hoped to have a chance of studying it.'

Over dinner, Philip lingered at her table several times, his hand straying discretely to the lining of her shawl.

At the end of the evening the guests began to leave, and Monica remained, alone at her table, appearing as if she were absorbed in her book.

Grant and Teresa had long ago given up playing 'I Spy' and were leaning against each other, dozing, when the first couple got into their car and banged the doors shut.

Grant jumped into full consciousness. 'Here they come,' he whispered.

At length only three cars remained. 'I expect the owners are staying the night,' Teresa surmised.

'Probably.'

'I wish I was a fly on the wall in there,' said Teresa.

'If I were, I'd probably change into an elephant and sit on him,' replied Grant grimly.

Teresa chuckled. 'I can imagine it. He'd be crushed.' She became serious. 'He'll be taking her upstairs now.'

'I feel like galloping in and biffing him one.'

'Well, don't!'

'Why not? That's what he deserves.'

'I know, but we've got a greater purpose to achieve.'

'You'll have to remind me precisely what that is,' said Grant tersely.

'We're trying to find out what's going on,' Teresa reminded him patiently.

'But don't we know already? He poisons people with some weird concoction, and then does ghastly things around them while they're unconscious. What more is there to know?' Grant was seething. 'Teresa, my instincts are about to get the better of me. When I think of him flaunting himself around you, I want to break his neck, and I'm expected to sit here, thinking about what's happening to Monica right at this very moment.'

'Look, Grant,' said Teresa firmly, 'she's not going to drink that stuff.' She fell silent for a moment, and then added, 'But I do appreciate the strain you're under, and I'm very sorry indeed for my part in it.'

Grant took her hand. 'Thanks for that. It really helps.'

Hands clasped, they sat in silence.

Upstairs, Monica was sitting on Philip's sofa, pretending to sip from the glass of cordial that he had given her. Her shawl was spread on the back of the sofa, and one of Philip's hands was buried in the lining of it, while the other was fingering the sleeve of her blouse. It seemed to her that he was oblivious of her. She put her mind to working out how to reduce the level of the liquid in her glass without having to swallow any of it.

Then she devised a strategy. She wedged her glass between

her thighs, and used her spare arm to locate the wad of tissues that she had tucked under the waistband of her skirt. It was commonly her habit to store tissues in this way, and she was profoundly grateful that she had not made today an exception. She dropped a few on the floor, worked her foot round them to make a pad, picked up her glass, and surreptitiously poured some of its contents on to the pad. Then she used her foot again to edge the wet tissues under the sofa. So far, so good. She resumed her play of sipping.

More time passed. 'Would you like to have a look at my book now?' she asked.

Philip was startled out of his reverie. 'Book?'

'Yes, the one about the herbal concoctions.'

'Oh, yes... that book. I would certainly like to see it.'

Philip looked at each of his hands in turn, wondering which he could spare. She put her glass on the floor, and took the book from her bag. He took it in his blouse hand and placed it on his knee.

'Do you mind if I look at the view from your window?' Monica asked casually.

Philip looked at his shawl hand. It was safely attached to the satin. 'No, not at all.'

She stood up and sauntered across the room, stopping on the way to admire a plant. Skillfully she tipped some of the drink into its pot, until only half the original amount remained. The darkness outside was punctured only by spots of light from the outbuildings, and everything was quiet.

'It's very peaceful here,' she commented. 'Philip, this drink is superb. You *must* tell me what's in it.'

He jumped. 'I couldn't possibly do that. It's a secret.'

'But surely you could tell *me*. I promise I won't tell anyone else.'

Philip shook his head. She stepped towards the sofa, stumbled a little, and clutched at his knee.

'I feel a little strange,' she murmured.

He used his book hand to guide her on to the sofa saying

'You must be feeling tired. Finish up your drink and then you can relax here for a while.'

'I must use your bathroom first,' said Monica as sleepily as she could.

Philip had taken the precaution of freeing up the connecting door in advance of this encounter, and he led her through the bedroom to the bathroom.

Once inside, she secured the door, tipped the rest of her drink away, and sent a text to Teresa: OK so far. Have got rid of drink. After that she flushed the toilet, ran water in the basin, and then stumbled back through the bedroom to the sofa, sprawling herself on to it.

Outside in the car, Teresa read the text to Grant.

'Well done, Monica,' he said through gritted teeth. 'Now for the main action.'

Monica's was limp. Her eyes were closed. Philip checked her breathing. It was slow and deep. Good, the cordial had taken effect. He brought a blanket and spread it over her. She did not stir. And now the night was his – to spend exactly as he pleased.

First, the shawl… He buried his face in the satin lining and groaned with pleasure. Then he slung it across his shoulders, but that did little to provide satisfaction, as the satin touched only small areas of his skin. He placed it reverently on the back of the sofa, removed his cravat and his shirt, and again donned the shawl. The sensation of the satin on his naked torso was exquisite, and he was ecstatic.

Underneath the blanket Monica did not stir. Yet her eyes were not completely shut, and she could see much of what Philip was doing. As the scene unfolded, she observed that he was becoming more and more engrossed in acting out a sequence of fantasies – to which she was a silent witness. She could not imagine what they meant. Their significance was known only to him, but probably not even he was aware of it.

She thought of Teresa and Grant, waiting in the car, wondering what was happening now. But instinctively she knew it was paramount that at this stage she must not do anything to interrupt this bizarre play. She trusted that they would know she was still all right, and would not take action prematurely. Physically she felt quite comfortable. The sofa was firm and well upholstered, and the blanket was lightweight and warm.

Philip continued his pleasures. Monica would have preferred not to see any of this, but she had committed herself to the task of exposing him. She coped only by hanging on to the fact that if she and her friends were to have a chance of putting a stop to his inappropriate behaviour in relation to the women whom he selected, she had to learn more about exactly what was taking place and why.

She had no idea how much time passed. She dared not lift her arm to look at her watch.

Outside in the car, Teresa voiced her growing anxiety. 'It's been a long time.'

'Too long in my opinion,' Grant replied tersely. 'Let's go and storm the place.'

'No. We've got to trust that she's in control of the situation, and that she'll contact us if she needs us.'

'I don't think I can stick this out much longer. That man's unbalanced.'

Teresa was adamant. 'There's no alternative.'

From her prone position under the blanket, Monica could see that things were moving towards some kind of climax. She braced herself ready for action, and just as Philip seemed to be reaching the pinnacle of his activities, she sat bolt upright and said in her best imitation of a domineering teacher, 'Philip Thornton! What *do* you think you're doing?'

Philip looked as if he had been shot – right between the eyes. Then he seemed to lose consciousness, and he crashed to the floor, face down. Monica thought quickly. What should she do now?

She grabbed the blanket that had covered her, and put it over him. After that she took a glass to the bathroom and filled it with cold water. Then she made an incisive decision.

She tipped some of the water on the back of his neck and shook him, saying determinedly 'Wake up, Philip! I've some questions you have to answer.'

He trembled a little, but other than that he did not react.

She persisted. 'Come on, Philip!' Still there was no response. She increased the stress. 'I have some friends waiting in a car outside. If you don't get up now, I'll get them to join us.'

Philip sprang into action immediately. He pulled himself to a kneeling position in front of her and begged her not to do it.

Monica did not waver. 'I'll have to ring them. It's late, and they'll want to know what's happening.'

She took out her mobile phone and rang Teresa's. 'Everything's under control. He's about to confess.' Her voice was deliberately harsh. 'I'll be in touch again in about fifteen minutes.'

Philip made a choking sound.

Monica continued her interrogation. 'You have to tell me the truth of *everything. Now!*'

'I promise I haven't hurt anyone,' Philip gibbered in a squeaky voice.

'How do you know that? How can you be certain?'

'I've always been gentle and kind.'

Monica was relentless. 'Philip, knocking people out with a cocktail of goodness-knows-what is hardly gentle and kind.'

'But... but... I always made them comfortable afterwards.'

'That's no excuse. You were deceitful and duplicitous.'

Philip gathered himself and tried again. 'Every one of them agreed to come up here. My approach was always an invitation. I didn't force anybody.'

'But I bet no one knew what they were agreeing to. No one

knew what your invitation actually meant.'

Monica's determination to keep challenging him broke through his defences.

'I... I... I didn't give cordial to all of them. And... And the things I've done have been nearly always on my own.'

'Convince me,' said Monica, doing her best to effect a sneer.

Philip hesitated.

'Philip, there's no way out,' Monica informed him sternly.

He hung his head like a schoolboy. His mind filled with memories of miscreant classmates who had had to endure corporal punishment.

Monica spoke again. 'Who can let my friends in?'

Philip froze. 'Not in here,' he begged, wringing his hands desperately.

'Into the hotel.'

'Tell them to press the buzzer that's hidden under the sill to the left of the front door.'

Monica did as he directed. He pointed to an entry phone unit at the side of the door to the corridor. The unit activated, and Monica told Grant and Teresa to enter and then wait for her in the lounge downstairs.

After that, Philip slowly began to tell her the whole story – starting with his purchase of the buildings, his involvement in their transformation, and his discovery of the secret room. Monica listened carefully, interrupting only to ask precisely framed questions. Whenever he faltered, she put pressure on him to continue, insisting that he must be entirely truthful.

As the tale unfolded, she began to see what lay behind the polished exterior that Philip presented in his public life. He was confused and lonely. What little she learned about his family was enough to demonstrate that his childhood experience had been impoverished and isolating, and consequently he had no real grasp of what close relationship was about. However, she was careful to show nothing of her growing sense of compassion towards him. What he needed was firm handling and effective guidance. With perseverance this could lead to a way ahead, bringing balance into his life – a life that would no longer involve luring women into his distorted fantasies.

When at last she was sure that he had told her more or less everything, Monica said, 'I don't think that you have deliberately withheld anything, but remember, if more comes to mind, you *must* let me know.'

Philip nodded meekly.

Monica continued. 'Before I leave, we must agree the start of a way forward.'

Philip nodded again, saying nothing. His big eyes followed her every movement.

'Philip,' she asked quietly, 'how do you think you are going to make amends?'

'I… I don't know.'

'It's something we're going to have to think a lot about, then. Isn't it?'

His eyes averted her gaze.

'Philip, do you know the meaning of the word "remorse"?'

His shook his head mutely.

'In order to express true remorse, a perpetrator of harm must first understand what he has done wrong, and then he must demonstrate that he has a grasp of the impact of his wrongdoing upon the victim. He has to understand how the victim has been feeling, and he has to be able to acknowledge that and respond to it appropriately.'

Philip clutched his head. 'I don't know what you mean,' he moaned. 'I haven't done anything wrong.' He took a gulp of air. 'Everybody liked what I did. I know they did.'

Then slowly and deliberately Monica outlined her best threat.

'Philip, if you do not agree to do what I say, I promise that I will go to the local newspaper about what you have been doing in these rooms.'

Philip was already pale, but when he heard this, all colour drained completely from his face. 'You can't! You mustn't!'

he squeaked.

'I can, and I will, if you don't do what you have to.'

'All right then! I'll be your slave.'

'No, Philip, you won't be my slave. That won't help you or anybody else. You need to agree to a process which will guide you in the task of becoming a proper adult person.'

At this, Philip's panic diminished. Although he couldn't understand what was happening, it sounded as if instead of punishing him this woman was trying to help him in some way.

'There's to be no more of this luring women up here. If you're tempted, you mustn't do it. Instead you have to tell me about it. I'll be your friend, and help you into other interests. It's only when you have become a proper adult person that you'll be able to engage with women in a healthy balanced way. You'll enjoy getting to know them as people, and you'll come to value their companionship.'

Philip looked puzzled, but said nothing.

Monica went on. 'It's got very late. There's one more thing to do before I leave.'

Philip was bemused. There was already so much that he couldn't really grasp, and now she was demanding something else.

'As a start we'll draft a letter as if it's to one of the women you've misled.'

Philip was about to object, but the look on Monica's face silenced him. He found a large notebook and a pen, and handed them to her.

Monica shook her head. 'You have to be the one who writes it.'

Philip produced some sentences of scrawl and handed the result to her.

Monica read it aloud. 'Dear Maisie, Monica said I've got to say I'm sorry. I didn't know I was being bad. I hope you don't feel angry or upset with me. Regards, Philip.' Monica sucked her cheeks in, to prevent herself from smiling. She was about to make him try again, when she relented, saying 'I suppose this is a start.'

Philip said nothing. He felt confused and exhausted.

Monica stifled a yawn. 'It must be very late, and I'm tired. I'll go now. You don't have to come and let me out. I'll collect the others, and we'll make sure the front door is pulled shut properly as we leave. I'll be in touch some time over the next week.' She scowled at him. 'And don't get up to any nonsense!'

'I promise. I promise.' Philip's panic was rising again. Her demands were almost completely incomprehensible. He was very glad that she was going away, but at one and the same time he didn't want her to leave him – all alone. He wanted to push her out of his room, and he wanted to grab her and not let her go. But there was nothing he could say to communicate this, and when she left, he rushed through the connecting door into Room 7, dived into the bed and hid under the duvet.

Downstairs, Monica found Teresa and Grant dozing in the lounge. Each of them occupied an armchair. They had both taken off their shoes, and their feet shared the same coffee table.

Teresa jerked to full consciousness. 'How did it go? I want to know absolutely everything.'

'So do I,' said Grant, 'but first I think we should concentrate on getting ourselves home.' He slipped his feet into his shoes.

'You're absolutely right, Grant,' agreed Monica, 'and I want to get out of here as soon as possible. Where we got up to this evening was fine, but I don't want to have to encounter Philip again tonight.' As they made their way to the car, she added grimly, 'Teresa, I was entirely right in thinking he has involved more women. There have been *many* more.'

Minutes later, Grant was turning the car out on to the road, and soon they were deep in discussion as Monica recounted what had taken place. They arrived back at Teresa and Grant's house when there was still much to cover, and they decided that Monica should stay the night so that they could continue the following morning.

Over lunch the next day, Teresa expressed concern.

'Monica, I think you've set yourself up for what could be a long and thorny responsibility.'

'It was the only way I could think of handling the situation at the time, but I agree.'

Grant was thoughtful. 'I think it's very unwise for it to be something that's only between him and you.'

'So do I,' agreed Teresa.

'But he was terrified at the thought of you being involved,' Monica pointed out.

'I've taken that in,' said Grant, 'but that doesn't mean we have to protect him from having that feeling. Monica, I can see exactly why you took the route you did, but we've got to broaden things out very soon.'

'At least he's in no doubt that two friends are in it with me,' said Monica.

'Maybe that'll be sufficient,' mused Teresa.

'I don't agree,' said Grant firmly. 'If he's capable of weaving the kind of fantasies we're now aware of, given time, he could write us out of the picture...'

'... unless we're in it more obviously,' Teresa finished for him.

'Exactly.'

Monica considered this. She could see that Grant was right, but for some reason she found herself worrying about how Philip would take it. 'I'll have to think it through...' Her voice trailed off.

Teresa looked at her sharply. 'Unless you keep a clear objective grasp of the overall situation, you run the risk of becoming enmeshed in Philip's warped point of view.'

'But he confided really personal things to me,' Monica reminded her.

'That doesn't mean he's suddenly fixed,' Grant pointed out. 'You kept him on the spot, and he had no choice but to tell you. You did really well, but please don't start feeling sorry for him.'

'Well, actually, I do,' Monica admitted. 'He's so obviously

lonely and isolated. It's just that the way he went about trying to ease it was wrong.'

Teresa took her friend by the shoulders and shook her gently. 'We've got to take into account the effect of it on all those people he lured into his mess. You faced him with that last night, and we have to keep up the pressure. If you can't do it, then Grant and I must take over the task.'

Monica shook her head as if to clear it. 'Where on earth was I drifting off to? You're absolutely right. Let's get down to business. We've got to agree a plan that will keep him on track, and it has to involve a lot more than just him and me having chats.'

'Welcome back, Monica,' said Grant. 'You'd got me a bit worried there.'

Monica smiled across at him. 'There's something else we haven't covered yet.'

'Go on.'

'We should put more thought into that drink – the cordial. What if there's something in it that really shouldn't be? Do you think we should be involving the police?'

'That's certainly been on my mind,' Grant replied slowly.

'I must confess that it hasn't been on mine,' said Teresa.

'He refused point blank to tell me what was in it,' Monica reminded them. 'But of course that might merely be because he wants it to remain a secret, and not because it contains something dangerous.'

'Since I'm the only one of the three of us who's been under its influence, maybe I should talk again about how I felt afterwards,' Teresa suggested.

'Can you include what Carrie told you about it, too?' Monica asked.

Teresa looked uncertain. 'I promised her I wouldn't say anything.' She paused for a moment before continuing. 'But from what I learned, I guess her reaction was quite similar to mine, although I think hers lasted longer.'

'I had the impression that the cordial is sometimes made

available to dinner guests,' said Monica.

'You're right,' Teresa agreed. 'I'd forgotten about that. But how would that work? He wouldn't want guests to be passing out over dinner.'

'Could be something to do with the dilution,' Grant suggested. 'If the effect of the dining version is equivalent to a glass of wine, then it would be unremarkable.'

'I can't say that the stuff I had was like drinking neat spirits,' said Teresa. 'I would certainly have noticed with the first sip.'

'But it could have an equivalent effect, without tasting the same,' Monica pointed out.

'The muzzy head I had in the morning cleared relatively quickly,' Teresa mused. 'I didn't feel as if I had a hangover... but I did feel a bit as if I'd been drugged.'

'I think that on balance I wouldn't want to involve the police at this stage,' Grant decided.

Teresa nodded, and Monica said, 'I'll go along with that.'

There was a pause, and then slow smile spread across Grant's face. 'I've had an idea.'

'Tell us,' Teresa demanded.

Grant savoured his thought for a minute or two before beginning. 'Teresa, you remember how much we enjoyed the meal at *Field Fare*?'

'Of course I do. The food was superb, and we had quite a lot of fun, too. Why do you ask?'

There was a twinkle in Grant's eyes as he replied. 'I have it in mind to take you there on a pretty regular basis from now on.'

As Teresa's eyes met his she exclaimed, 'Ah! You mean that Philip should be given the information that it was you and I who were sitting outside in the car...'

'Precisely! And maybe that's all that needs to be done at the moment. He'll never be in any doubt that we are in close communication with Monica, and he won't be able to pretend to himself that his relationship with Monica is secret. Naturally, we can mention her name from time to time as he passes our

129

table…'

'That's a masterly plan,' said Monica admiringly. 'I feel very comfortable with it.'

'Maybe sometimes the three of us should dine there together as well,' Teresa suggested.

'Perfect!' Monica agreed.

Chapter Twenty

Monica's next meeting with Philip was in his office – with the 'Engaged' sign in place and the door shut. When she told him who her friends were, he was beside himself. He squirmed and twisted on his chair until Monica began to worry that his physical distortions might result in some injury. However, she managed not to show concern or impede his struggles. Instead she went on to make it clear that Grant and Teresa would be dining at *Field Fare* on a regular basis, and that she would sometimes join them. She told him that he would have no control over that at all, and that he would have to ensure that they were always fitted in.

With the threat of his exploits being reported in the local paper hanging over him, Philip made no attempt to object. Such exposure was certain to lead to the loss of everything he had created, and that would surely be the end of him. His only option was to go along with everything that Monica said, hoping that there would be something better beyond. However, at this moment everything felt excruciating. Inwardly he tried to comfort himself with thoughts of opening up the secret room and spending his free time there. But the room was no longer secret! *She* knew all about it, and her friends did, too. Being in it could never be the same as it had before... Her voice penetrated the jumble of thoughts that were terrifying him.

'Philip, have you had any ideas of luring women since we last spoke?'

'Er... no.'

'I don't believe you,' Monica snapped.

Philip felt as if she had hit him, and leaning on his desk, he hid his head under his arms.

The voice continued relentlessly. 'Exactly what were you

planning?'

There was no way out except to tell her, thought Philip. But what would that mean? He turned his face towards her, and keeping his eyes tight shut said, 'There's one who comes every few weeks. She's different...' Here his voice trailed off.

'What do you mean?' asked Monica curiously. Her tone was no longer harsh. 'You didn't tell me about her before.'

'We look at the natural history records together, and then we sleep.' He hesitated, before adding, 'I feed her on chocolates – the ones with rum-flavoured marzipan inside.'

Monica noted that when he mentioned the chocolates, his voice took on child-like tones. 'Tell me about the sleeping,' she directed.

Philip's eyes were still screwed up tightly. 'We snuggle up.'

'What do you do?'

Philip's eyes opened suddenly. 'I told you,' he insisted.

'Oh!' Monica's response was entirely involuntary. She felt something melt inside her as she imagined the scene.

Remembering that she must keep her mind on the task in hand, she was resolute in making herself think about his other kinds of encounter before responding further.

'Philip,' she said carefully, 'you must let her know that you won't be able to see her for a while.'

'How long?' Philip asked in a pathetic voice.

'At least six months,' Monica told him firmly.

Philip was horrified at the prospect. To be deprived of Amanda's company for that length of time was insupportable. It wasn't fair! Surely there could be no objection to how he had related to her, so why insist on putting a stop to his contact with her? How could Monica do this to him? He opened his mouth to object but was deterred by an unfamiliar feeling that he couldn't quite identify.

Monica observed his struggles silently. She knew that it was important to give him time to feel the impact of her statement. She would wait until he was ready to say something.

Even though Philip had a very strong internal resistance to what Monica had laid down, he was surprised to find that somehow there seemed to be a kernel of sense in what she had said. He couldn't quite grasp precisely why that was, but he had some inklings. If he didn't see Amanda at all for a while, he would be relieved of the stress and worry of the possibility of her coming too often. Added to that, he knew that if he let Amanda come, he would find it impossible to conceal the visit from Monica, and she would demand to know all the details. This latter thought alone filled him with such horror that any idea of subversion fled from his mind.

He found himself saying 'She books by e-mail. Next time, I'll let her know I can't offer a room because I'm having some refurbishment done.' He drew himself up and tried hard to look straight at Monica.

At that moment Monica could see in front of her a fragment of the man that Philip could become. 'Yes,' she said slowly. 'Personal refurbishment.'

Overall, the 'Philip' project advanced satisfactorily during the summer months, although during the early stages there were some challenging times for both Monica and Philip. When his reaction to the initial shock of Monica's confrontation had receded a little, Philip's old habits of planning scenarios to fit his fantasies continued unabated. At first he was tempted to keep much of this from her, and he spent time rehearsing how to appear as if he were telling her everything, while actually withholding most of it.

He found that the fantasies were evolving and changing, so that some of their content was quite different from what he had already been forced to divulge. Surely he could keep these new experiences to himself, he thought. But he found Monica to be an indefatigable adversary in his attempts to withhold essential information from her, and that he could not find any way of subverting the process and defeating her. Time and time again, he discovered that she had an almost uncanny ability of detecting his slightest deviation from complete truth. How did she do it? he wondered.

Alone, he would practise lying by omission while observing his face minutely in the bathroom mirror. Yet even when he was certain that he had perfected the art, almost straight away she would demonstrate that she could see through it. In fact there were many times when it felt as if she could see right inside him, and that was more than he could bear. But he *had* to bear it, because he had no power to deceive her.

Being faced with the grinding ongoing reality of knowing that there was no way out of telling her was awful enough, but the actual process of verbalising these secrets to her was excruciating. Philip would sweat profusely, his voice would become barely a whisper, and his legs would feel so weak that it was necessary to sit down. On occasions, he felt so dizzy that he feared he would faint.

There were many times when he felt sharp stabs of anger rise up in him because of what Monica was putting him through. At such times he was blind to any awareness of the bad effects of his secret behaviour towards women. He would seethe inwardly about Monica's unfairness. Why couldn't he do what he wanted? His life had been fine until she came along!

His intense fear of public exposure continued to plague him. He never had any doubt that he could not endure such punishment. The only way out of this whole mess was to face the impossible task of forcing himself to be completely honest with Monica.

However, fearing that if he told her about his anger towards her she would punish him, it was quite some time before Philip said anything about it. But one day it occurred to him that all this time she must have detected some signs. Why was it that she had never mentioned it? She was so astute, so vigilant and so intuitive, and it was impossible that it had escaped her scrutiny. When he eventually raised the subject with her, he spoke about his anger in a different kind of situation, and then watched her reaction very carefully.

He made a start by telling her how he hated the way he had always to be very exact about his tax returns, and that he felt angry with the Inland Revenue.

Monica chuckled. 'I imagine there are plenty of people who have those feelings.'

Philip felt both reassured and irritated. His response to the latter feeling was to clench his teeth and mutter 'stupid woman' under his breath. Yet in addition he felt a kind of panic rise in this throat. He swallowed, and then managed to say 'You... don't... understand.'

At this, Monica became serious. 'Philip, I think I do. I think you're trying to talk to me about something even more important than the Inland Revenue.'

This punctured Philip's panic, and he suddenly felt exhausted. 'I'll tell you later,' he mumbled evasively.

To his surprise, Monica did not press him, and instead merely commented in a neutral way, 'Yes, I'm sure you will.'

This had been the beginning of a new phase. Now Philip made several brief references to his anger towards her. At first he was very surprised and puzzled to find that although she always acknowledged what he said, she never pushed him to say more. Slowly he began to trust the consistency of her responses, and gradually he became more daring about telling her about his anger towards her for putting him through torture.

As time went on, Philip found to his amazement that there was a small but palpable shift in how he felt about the enforced sharing of his life. Although still very challenging, the process of talking to Monica about his innermost thoughts became not quite so terrible for him.

Eventually the day came when he found himself *wanting* to tell her about something new that had come into his mind. He had been cleaning his bathroom when he had been taken over by something so powerful that he had dropped the new bottle of cream cleaner in the bath, where a liberal quantity of its contents escaped. The sudden lemony smell of the first squirt had been the start of it. It had been a complete surprise, as he habitually used the unscented kind, and now so much had escaped he felt that he was being engulfed in a tidal wave of lemon. The state that took him over was inextricably linked to that lemon smell. For a moment or two, he was certain that his mother was in the room. Yet that could not be the case! She had died a long time ago. Then it was as if she had said something. What was it? But try as he might, he could not grasp it.

After this, he felt extremely tired. He went to his sitting room and lay down on the sofa. It was not long before he felt an urgent desire to speak to Monica. Although unmistakable, the feeling was entirely unfamiliar to him. How strange, he thought. Despite its newness, it did not occur to him to question its validity. He was filled with a longing, so intense that his whole chest ached with it. Today was Monday, and his next meeting with her was not until Thursday. What should he do?

Then he remembered that she had told him to contact her by text if he found himself in difficulty. He had never imagined that he would want to speak to her between their meetings, and until this moment he had thrust the offer out of his consciousness.

He stood up and fetched his mobile phone from his jacket. His hands were shaking a little as he tapped out a brief message. Thank goodness her number was in the phone book of his mobile. After sending the message he felt a little calmer, but this was only a temporary lull, and it was soon replaced by extreme agitation. He wanted an immediate response! How long would it be before she replied? How could he endure the waiting?

The minutes crawled past, each seeming like an hour. Philip was unable to do anything but wait. Then at last a text came back to say that she would ring him soon. Relief! After that he found he could return to the bathroom and clean up the mess. By the time he had finished, his bath was sparkling. He passed more time by looking through the magazine sections of Saturday's newspapers. There wasn't anything of particular interest, but this didn't seem to matter.

Then his phone rang, and he picked it up immediately.

'Hello, Philip.'

The familiar sound of her voice was deeply reassuring. Straight away he told her what was on his mind. 'Something happened when I was in the bathroom,' he began.

As he recounted the experience, Monica remained silent apart from making a number of small affirmative sounds, and when he had finished, she said very little.

'I'm glad you contacted me. It was exactly the right thing to do.'

'I know,' Philip agreed confidently. He wavered only for a moment before adding 'I won't keep you. I can get on now.' And he rang off. He felt quite calm, and had a curious feeling that he could only describe as having something pleasantly solid inside. A fleeting image of a large pot of double cream passed through his mind and vanished. It held no attraction for him at all.

There were quite a number of times over the whole summer period when intensive discussion about Philip between Monica, Teresa and Grant was required. As this progressed, the three friends were surprised to discover that applying their minds in this way was leading to a deepening of their own awareness and perceptions. Clearly the process of devising the best way of helping Philip was having a positive impact all round, and this was not something that they had expected.

Chapter Twenty-one

September came, and Monica began her course in computer science. Grant and Teresa saw a new level of vibrance shine from her personality. Her eagerness and enthusiasm were very apparent. Grant and Teresa took over her involvement in monitoring Philip's situation. By that time, he was completely accepting of their help, and had reached the position where he almost looked forward to the times when they dined at *Field Fare*. On occasion he had even consulted them about certain dishes that he was considering adding to the menu. Grant occasionally attended conferences abroad, and he always tried to bring back information about local delicacies and their preparation.

Philip continued to add to his collection of old recipes, and paid a home economics student to spend time cataloguing them. He planned to contact the probation service to see if he could help a young person into work, by offering some training in his kitchen. This idea had come entirely from Philip himself, but he discussed it in detail with Teresa and Grant.

Although at times Philip still found himself struggling with inappropriate impulses, he now had no doubt that following them through was of no help to him at all, and could well be of harm to others. He began to wish that there was a way of making amends to those he had used for his gratification, but he could not work out what to do. He remembered little or nothing about the people he had involved, and approaching anyone he did remember might not lead to a helpful outcome. He kept these thoughts to himself for a long time, but when at last he did talk to Grant and Teresa about them, a way forward presented itself.

Without saying anything to Philip of her intentions, Teresa

raised the subject with Carrie at her next hair appointment.

'You remember how I said I was going to do some investigation on the subject of Philip Thornton and *Field Fare*?' she began.

'Yes, I do. I hope you haven't said anything about me,' Carrie added hurriedly.

'Of course not,' Teresa assured her. 'It's quite a long story, and I won't go into details. Suffice it to say that Philip Thornton is quite a reformed character.'

Carrie stood like a statue for a moment, before continuing working on Teresa's hair. 'I'm glad to hear that,' she said carefully.

'For example, he's about to give temporary employment in the kitchen to a young man who's on probation.'

Carrie was impressed, and said so. She relaxed a little. 'Anything else?'

Teresa hesitated, but decided to go ahead. 'He wants to make amends to anyone he might have harmed. One problem is that he can't remember who he was with, and the other is that he doesn't want to risk causing further distress.'

Carrie was stunned. The comb she was using slipped out of her fingers and on to the floor. 'Are you *sure*?' she asked in sheer disbelief.

Teresa reached down, picked up the comb and pressed it into Carrie's hand. 'Keep working,' she said in a low voice.

Carrie used the comb with mechanical strokes.

Teresa went on. 'Carrie, do you have any ideas about what he could do?'

Carrie's thoughts were whirling. Only weeks ago she had remembered something of what had happened in Mr Thornton's room, but she didn't want to say anything about it. He had helped her to start her training earlier than she might have, but it had been for the wrong reasons, and somehow inside her that had tainted her feelings about her success. She didn't want anything more from him, but she would certainly like that bad feeling to go away.

Concerned about Carrie's silence, Teresa asked, 'I hope you don't feel I've put you under some kind of pressure.'

Carrie shook her head. Encouraged by Teresa's sensitivity towards her, she said, 'I want to talk to you, but I can't do it here.'

'Of course. When do you finish work today? How about meeting for a coffee afterwards?'

Carrie sighed with relief. 'I finish a bit early this afternoon, so I'll be leaving here soon after four.'

'How about a quiet corner at "The Currant Bun" at four thirty?'

Teresa could see in the mirror that Carrie's face had broken into a smile.

The coffee was hot and comforting. Carrie put her hands on the sides of the large cup as she spoke.

'I don't want to have this feeling that Mr Thornton helped me in my hairdressing career for the wrong reasons.'

Teresa, impressed by Carrie's honesty and integrity, said, 'Let's think about it, and see if we can come up with something.'

They sipped their coffee in silence for a while.

Then Teresa asked, 'How would you feel if I got him to write to you?'

Carried looked worried. 'I don't know about that. He'd have to remember my name.' She shuddered. 'It's too personal.'

'He wouldn't need to know your name,' Teresa pressed kindly. 'All he needs to know is that his wrong actions have affected you, and he would be writing to apologise, in full.'

Carrie wavered. 'But... he helped me... The extra work and the extra money helped me.'

'But you know it was because of something wrong that he did,' Teresa prompted gently. Why was Carrie now trying to see Philip in a better light? she wondered. This reminded her a little of how on the night of Philip's exposure, Monica had later slipped into a state where for a short while her sympathy towards his difficulties had become uppermost.

Teresa was about to say something else when she realised that Carrie was deep in thought, and instead she waited.

When at last Carrie spoke, Teresa was profoundly grateful that she had not interrupted her reflective state.

'When I was growing up, we never had much money,' she began. She took a deep breath. 'My dad wasn't easy to get on with. He had a fearsome temper that took a hold of him at the drop of a hat.' She dropped her head between her shoulders as she thought of this. Then she pulled herself upright again and went on. 'I used to be quite scared of him. But one thing I could always be sure about was that he would do everything he could to make sure I got the most from my schooling. When I had a chance of going to school camp, he took on extra work to earn more money so that I could go.'

'Carrie, I'm very sorry you were frightened of your own father,' said Teresa sympathetically.

'Mum explained to me about his temper, but I was still scared.' Carrie's voice was barely a whisper. 'But I know my dad's a good man because he did everything he could to...' Here her voice trailed off. But when she spoke again, she sounded quite different. 'He must have known I was scared. I used to run and hide behind the sofa. Maybe he felt guilty, and that's why he helped with the money for school camp. Going to school camp was a great experience, but...'

'Mm...' Teresa mused. 'I can see exactly what you're saying.'

'And going to the hairdressing course early was the perfect way forward for me, but there was something wrong about what Mr Thornton did. I was happy about what he offered – just like I was happy about Dad paying for school camp...'

'... but you didn't want the wrong side of how these things came about,' Teresa finished for her.

Carrie nodded her head vigorously.

'How do you get on with your father now?' asked Teresa.

'Great!' Carrie replied. 'I won't stand any of his nonsense any more. He seems to respect me for that, and I can see that Mum likes the change.'

'Well then, let's think of a way of making things right in this other situation,' Teresa encouraged.

'Mr Thornton can write a letter that says he knows he's been doing wrong things, and that he wished he hadn't, and that he's not going to do them any more. Then he can write about some proper things he's planning to do in the future.'

'I like that. Can I tell him?'

Carrie looked straight into Teresa's eyes. 'Yes, tell him, but remember you're not to say my name.'

After this they chatted about hairdressing, and Teresa took a great interest in Carrie's plans and dreams for the future.

That night, as she lay in bed, Teresa thought about Carrie's reactions to their conversation. It had been so interesting to discover that there was a connection between her past relationship with her father and her feelings about what Philip had done. Maybe Monica's temporary slide into sympathy towards Philip's situation had a similar root? But surely it couldn't be to do with her parents. Teresa had met Monica's mother and father and had found them to be kind, supportive people. No, it could not be their behaviour that had been a problem.

Yet there was something niggling away in Teresa's mind. Why had Monica never had a serious boyfriend? She had no apparent difficulty in enjoying friendships with men, but a more intimate relationship was something that, as far as Teresa was aware, she had never had. Teresa thought about Monica's relationship with Grant. There were no clues there, as she related to him with an obvious and genuine ease that was characteristic of her friendships with other men. She resolved to do her best to raise the matter with Monica when they next spent time together.

Chapter Twenty-two

When Philip heard from Teresa that there was a young woman who would be helped by receiving a letter from him, he was earnest in his determination to produce something appropriate straight away. That evening, he took out writing paper and a pen, and made a start. He concentrated very hard, and little by little he created something that he felt was right. It took him several more evenings before he thought he had perfected it.

Now he was left with a considerable dilemma. This letter was very private, and he did not want anyone to read it, except of course the woman for whom it was intended. However there was no way of getting it to her, because to him she was anonymous. What should he do? Teresa or Monica would be certain to insist on checking the letter through, but he did not want it to be altered in any way. This letter contained the evidence of his heartfelt remorse, and it was private between him and the woman who represented those he had wronged.

In the end he decided to approach Grant with his dilemma, hoping that he would understand. He sealed the letter in an envelope, and then wrote a covering note to go with it in a larger envelope, which he addressed to Grant.

Teresa's next meeting with Monica was very fruitful. After telling Monica a little of what had passed between her and Carrie, she found that Monica became eager to confide something that she had never told to any of her friends.

'When you were telling me about the problems Carrie had had with her father, I could see straight away how that had affected the way she was with Philip. It only took another minute or two before it dawned on me that Philip had been reminding me of an uncle I saw quite frequently when I was young – an uncle whose behaviour towards me wasn't quite right.'

'Goodness!' Teresa exclaimed.

'I sometimes had to go to his house for a while after school. I felt really uncomfortable around him.'

'Did you tell your parents?'

'I said something to Mum, but she told me he was well meaning, and that she was sure he hadn't meant to upset me. I know that in the grand scheme of things what he did was lightweight, but I didn't like it.'

'And that's what counts,' said Teresa firmly. 'If you didn't like it, then someone should have helped you.'

'I had to keep going back there and put up with how he was. Mum told me it was good of him to help by having me.'

'Oh dear,' Teresa sympathised. 'Your mum's a really nice person, but she got that completely wrong, didn't she?'

'She certainly did,' Monica agreed.

Teresa noticed that the colour had drained from Monica's face. She wanted to ask more, but she was hesitant. She didn't want her to feel that she was probing into her private life, but she was concerned for her. At length she said, 'I'd like to ask you something else, but you don't have to answer.'

Monica smiled. 'I know I don't have to. What is it?'

Teresa decided to be completely direct. 'I've never known you to have a boyfriend. Do you think it's something to do with what happened with your uncle?'

Monica winced.

'I'm sorry. I shouldn't have asked.'

'It isn't that,' Monica told her. 'I'll explain. I did once have a boyfriend. It was a long time ago. I was nineteen, and he was quite a bit older – nearly thirty, I think.'

Teresa was very surprised. 'Why haven't you mentioned him before?'

'I didn't want to think about him. You'll soon understand. I don't want to go into a lot of detail. Suffice it to say that there were things he did that reminded me of that uncle. I didn't

144

realise it at the time, though. Mum thought he was great, and she put quite a bit of pressure on me to make a go of the relationship. She got on well with him, and couldn't understand why I backed away from him. He had a good income and lived in a house he had bought a year or so before we met. It wasn't all that far from where Mum and Dad lived...'

'Now you've told me this, I *do* understand.'

'After that relationship, I made the decision that I wanted men in my life as friends, but never as potential partners.'

'Can I ask another question?' asked Teresa tentatively.

Monica nodded.

'Have you ever talked to your mum about this since?'

Monica shook her head. 'Mum and I get on fine together. I don't want to upset her.'

'But... What about your life?'

Monica smiled brightly. 'I've got a step nearer to what I really want. The course is great, and I'll make sure I use it to get me where I want to be in my career.'

'Monica, I think you're missing something. Put it this way... I enjoy my work, but it can't stand in place of the relationship I have with Grant. And see what a mess I got into when I was trying to cover up the fact that I was missing him.'

'I'm so glad you told me what was going on at *Field Fare*.'

'Yes, indeed, and it resulted in my getting the help I sorely needed. You've been great. Perhaps in time you'll realise I'm trying to give you the help that *you* need. Think about it.'

Monica shut her eyes. 'I know I'm hiding,' she admitted, 'but it's the only way I know of keeping safe.'

'Is it okay for me to tell Grant what you've told me?'

'No! Er... I mean... I'd find that difficult.... but, er... yes.'

'I'm sure he'd want to help.'

'That's just it. If he's kind to me about it, I'll probably start crying.'

'Maybe that's exactly what needs to happen.' Teresa touched her friend's arm. 'By the way, I've got a nice fantasy of you coming across someone while you're studying, and later finding you're really suited to each other.'

Monica looked very worried. 'But I can't have anything like that happening! The only way I could get away from him would be by leaving the course I love so much.'

'Look, it hasn't happened yet, and if it does, it will be after you've softened up a bit. You'll see.'

Monica relaxed visibly. 'So long as you don't expect miracles,' she warned.

Teresa noticed that a tinge of pink was creeping back into her friend's cheeks. 'We'll take it a step at a time,' she promised.

Chapter Twenty-three

Grant did not recognise the handwriting on the envelope. Puzzled, he slit it open. Inside was a note and another envelope. He read through the note, opened the envelope and read the letter inside.

'Good one, Philip!' he murmured.

Just then, Teresa came into the room. 'Oh, you've opened that letter,' she remarked. 'Who is it from?'

Grant did not reply straight away. Instead he went and put his arms round her. 'Our fledgling has taken some big strides of late,' he told her.

Teresa was mystified. 'You're talking in riddles.'

'It's Philip's response to the task of showing true remorse for the harm he has perpetrated to womankind.'

'Let me see.'

'He asked me not to show it to either you or Monica, and on this occasion, I'm willing to go along with his request. I promise you, the letter's flawless. I'll seal it up again, and when you next see Carrie, you can ask her if she'd like to see it.'

* * * * *

And the recipe for the cordial has remained a secret

* * * * *

Miranda by Mirabelle Maslin

ISBN 978-0-9558936-5-0   £6.99

Newly unemployed, Miranda is feeling directionless and dejected. Then she encounters Kate, a former work colleague. Kate is now facing redundancy. Their friendship is rekindled, and as the two women share their problems and dilemmas, they begin to confide about experiences that have affected their lives.

This is the first book in a series of self-help fiction titles.

By reading about the lives of fictional characters, the reader learns much about how to unravel present day problems. The understanding of stresses that began in childhood years casts light on why the characters are struggling with the difficulties that they are having now.

Order from your local bookshop, amazon.co.uk or the augurpress website at www.augurpress.com

Lynne by Mirabelle Maslin

ISBN 978-0-9558936-6-7   £6.99

Victimised by the new office manager and worried about her mother's health, Lynne feels at a very low ebb. When she decides to be more open with her mother about her concerns, she is surprised to find that they both benefit.

This is the second book in a series of self-help fiction titles.

Order from your local bookshop, amazon.co.uk or the augurpress website at www.augurpress.com

Also available from Augur Press

The Poetry Catchers by Pupils from Craigton Primary School	£7.99	978-0-9549551-9-9
Beyond the Veil by Mirabelle Maslin	£8.99	0-9549551-4-5
Fay by Mirabelle Maslin	£8.99	0-9549551-3-7
Emily by Mirabelle Maslin	£8.99	978-0-9549551-8-2
Miranda by Mirabelle Maslin	£6.99	978-0-9558936-5-0
Lynne by Mirabelle Maslin	£6.99	978-0-9558936-6-7
Hemiplegic Utopia: Manc Style by Lee Seymour	£6.99	978-0-9549551-7-5
Carl and other writings by Mirabelle Maslin	£5.99	0-9549551-2-9
Letters to my Paper Lover by Fleur Soignon	£7.99	0-9549551-1-0
On a Dog Lead by Mirabelle Maslin	£6.99	978-0-9549551-5-1
Poems of Wartime Years by W N Taylor	£4.99	978-0-9549551-6-8
Now Is Where We Are by Hilary Lissenden	£6.99	978-0-9558936-7-4
The Fifth Key by Mirabelle Maslin	£7.99	978-0-9558936-0-5
The Candle Flame by Mirabelle Maslin	£7.99	978-0-9558936-1-2
Mercury in Dental Fillings by Stewart J Wright	£5.99	978-0-9558936-2-9
The Voice Within by Catherine Turvey	£5.99	978-0-9558936-3-6
The Supply Teacher's Surprise by Mirabelle Maslin	£5.99	978-0-9558936-4-3
Tracy by Mirabelle Maslin	£6.95	0-9549551-0-2

Ordering: Postage and packing – £1.00 per title
By post   Delf House, 52, Penicuik Road, Roslin, EH25 9LH UK
Online   www.augurpress.com   (credit cards accepted)
Cheques payable to Augur Press. Prices and availability subject to change without notice. When placing your order, please mention if you do not wish to receive any additional information.

www.augurpress.com

Laughter   Soul
Joy
Sadness   Smiles

THE VOICE WITHIN

Pain

Beat

Tears   Pulse

CATHERINE TURVEY

Happiness   Love

Mirabelle Maslin

tracy

from the author of Beyond the Veil

POETRY catchers
Poems by Cramston Primary Pupils

Mirabelle Maslin
ON A DOG LEAD

Mercury in Dental Fillings

An information booklet compiled by
Stewart J Wright BDS

The impact of mercury on health.
Safe removal of dental mercury,
and the use of safe options
for restoration of teeth.

Letters to my Paper Lover
FLEUR SOIGNON

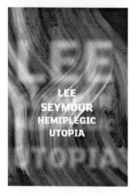

LEE
SEYMOUR
HEMIPLEGIC
UTOPIA

Mirabelle Maslin
CARL AND OTHER WRITINGS

Poems of Wartime Years
W N Taylor

The Supply Teacher's Surprise
Mirabelle Maslin

Now Is Where We Are
Hilary Lissenden

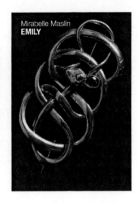

This is a trilogy

Lightning Source UK Ltd.
Milton Keynes UK
UKOW050611100312

188676UK00001B/34/P